Enid Blyton

SUMMER ADVENTURE STORIES

Look out for all of these enchanting story collections

by *Enid Blyton*

Enid Blyton
SUMMER ADVENTURE STORIES

Hodder
Children's
Books

HODDER CHILDREN'S BOOKS

This collection first published in Great Britain in 2019
by Hodder & Stoughton

1 3 5 7 9 10 8 6 4 2

A CIP catalogue record for this book is available from the British Library.

ISBN 978 1 444 94732 8

Printed and bound in Great Britain by Clays Ltd, Elcograf S.p.A.

The paper and board used in this book are made from
wood from responsible sources.

Hodder Children's Books
An imprint of Hachette Children's Group
Part of Hodder & Stoughton
Carmelite House
50 Victoria Embankment
London EC4Y 0DZ

An Hachette UK Company
www.hachette.co.uk
www.hachettechildrens.co.uk

Contents

The Silver Merman

The Silver Merman

JOHN WAS down by the seashore with his cousin Ella. He had been busy building sandcastles when suddenly he noticed that Ella was crying.

'What's the matter, Ella?' he asked, throwing down his spade, and running over to her.

'I have lost my lovely ring,' she sobbed.

'Where did you lose it?' asked John. 'Let's go and hunt for it. I'm sure it won't take long to find.'

'It's no use,' said Ella, drying her eyes. 'I lost it when I was out in the boat this morning. It fell off my finger as I was trailing my hand in the water, and before I could do anything, I saw it sinking down to the bottom of the sea.'

'If only I knew the way there, I'd go and hunt for

your ring,' said John. 'But I would drown if I went deep into the water.'

'Of course you would, silly,' said Ella, smiling. 'Carry on building castles, and forget about my ring!'

John went off and thought hard as he dug in the sand.

'I'm sure I'd find that ring if I could find someone to guide me under the sea,' he said to himself.

'Well, I'll take you if you like!' said a sweet voice near him. John looked up in surprise. He saw a fairy sitting on a rock, with long hair blowing in the wind.

'I've never seen a fairy before!' he cried in delight. 'Are you really a fairy?'

'Yes, really,' she answered. 'I'm on my way to visit my sister Pinkity, who married a merman. I heard what you said, as I was flying by, and I wondered if you'd like to come with me.'

'Oh, I would!' cried John. 'Do please take me.'

'Come along then,' said the fairy, holding out her hand. 'My name's Sylfai. What's yours?'

4

'John,' said the little boy. 'That's my cousin Ella over there. She lost her ring in the waves, and I want to go down to the bottom of the sea so that I can look for it.'

Sylfai led him into the water and it splashed over his socks. 'Oh dear, I'll get wet!' he said. 'I won't drown, will I?'

'Oh, I forgot,' said Sylfai. 'I must rub you with a sea spell, so that you can walk beneath the water safe and dry. What a good thing you reminded me!'

She put her hands in the water and then made an outline round John's body, singing some strange magic words as she did so.

'There! Now you'll be all right!' she said. 'Come along.'

They ran into the water, deeper and deeper, until John was right up to his waist. It wasn't at all difficult to walk in the sea, like it usually was. Soon he was up to his shoulders, and then suddenly his head went right under! But he didn't splutter or choke. It was just as easy breathing in the water as on the land. John thought it was really wonderful. Bright fish swam all around them, and beautiful seaweed floated everywhere.

'We've a long way to go, so we'll find a fish to ride on,' said Sylfai. She beckoned to a big codfish, and soon she and John were sitting comfortably on its back, racing through the water. Swish! Swish!

'I'm a little tired now,' said the codfish at last. 'Look, there's a crowd of jellyfish! Catch hold of the ribbons that hang down from them, and they'll carry you as far as you want to go! Don't worry, these ones won't sting.'

'Please take us to Pinkity, the Silver Merman's wife!' cried Sylfai. The jellyfish moved off quickly, and soon they arrived at a lovely cave, where a fairy sat combing out her long hair.

Sylfai let go of the jellyfish, and went to kiss her little sister. John followed her, feeling rather shy.

'Oh, Sylfai, how lovely to see you!' cried Pinkity.

'And who is this with you?'

'This is John,' said Sylfai. 'He's come to look for a lovely ring that his cousin has lost in the sea.'

'But the sea is such a big place – it would take him all his life to find it!' cried Pinkity. 'Never mind, John, maybe you could take her a pretty piece of coral instead.'

'Where's your husband?' asked Sylfai.

'Oh, he's gone to the Ocean Market,' said Pinkity. 'He'll be back soon, in time for tea.'

She set a cloth on a rock, and put a jug of pretty seaweed in the middle. Then she put out shells for plates, and cups made of pink coral. John couldn't think how anyone could drink out of a cup when there was water all around, but Sylfai said it was quite easy when you knew how! John was looking forward to trying.

Soon the meal was ready, and they took their places at the table. There was seaweed soup, pink and green jelly made from sea anemones, and starfish cakes. John was very hungry and, though he had never had such a strange meal before, he enjoyed it very much.

'Here's my husband!' cried Pinkity. John looked up, and saw a fine big merman swimming through the water. He had a tail like a fish, and gleamed like silver as he swam into the cave.

'Why, here's quite a party!' he said, chuckling. 'Who's our guest?'

'I'm John,' said John. 'I'm very pleased to meet you.'

'Same to you,' said the merman, and he sat down at the table, and helped himself to some jelly. He was very friendly, and he told John such funny stories about the fish and crabs that the little boy could hardly eat for laughing.

'I bought you a present at the market, Pinkity,' said the merman. 'It's something very special indeed! I paid a great many shells for it.'

'Oh, show me!' cried Pinkity. The merman opened his hand and showed them a beautiful ring. John cried out in astonishment!

'Why, it's the very ring that my cousin Ella lost! It really is!'

'Dear me, is that so?' asked the merman. 'It came down from the surface of the water this morning, and was taken to the market to be sold by the fish who found it.'

'Yes, and Ella lost hers this morning!' cried John. 'So it must be the same one. What a very peculiar thing!'

'Well, you must take it back to Ella,' said Pinkity. 'I couldn't keep it now I know that.'

'Oh, no,' said John, 'your husband bought it, and he must give it to you. I'll tell Ella, and I'm sure she'll be pleased when she knows you have got it.'

'No, you must take it,' said the merman.

But John wouldn't, no matter how they begged him to. He was quite sure Ella would rather Pinkity had it.

'I really ought to go back now,' he said. 'Ella will be worried.'

'I'll take you to the shore on one of my white horses!' said the merman. 'They go very fast indeed.'

He swam off, and soon came back with a beautiful horse, whose white mane streamed like foam in the water.

'I never knew that the white waves I saw rolling in to shore were really and truly the manes of horses!' said John in surprise.

The merman helped him up, and then sat on the horse behind him sideways, for his tail was rather awkward to manage on horseback.

'Goodbye!' called John, waving to Sylfai and Pinkity.

The white horse rose to the surface of the water and then, with its foamy mane just showing above the waves, began to gallop along swiftly.

Poor Ella had suddenly missed John, and was dreadfully worried about him. She was walking up and down by the sea, calling him. A host of little fish put their heads above the water and told her not to worry, but of course she couldn't understand a word they said. She wasn't under a sea spell, like John.

The white horse rushed out on the beach, and John jumped off. Before he could call goodbye and thank the merman, the horse had turned, and vanished once more. John went to look for Ella.

There she was, way along the beach, calling at the top of her voice, 'John, John, where are you?'

'Here I am!' called John, and he raced up to her.

'Oh, John, where have you been?' asked Ella. 'I have been so worried about you.'

'I've been to the bottom of the sea to look for your ring,' said John. 'And do you know, the Silver Merman had bought it for Pinkity! They wanted me to take it to you, but I said I knew you would much rather Pinkity had it, and I made them keep it.'

'What are you talking about?' said Ella. 'Don't tell stories, John! Nobody can go to the bottom of the sea, except divers.'

'But I did go!' said John, sticking his hands into his

pockets, as he always did when he was cross.

'Well, I don't believe you,' said Ella. 'You've just been hiding somewhere to give me a fright.'

'I haven't,' said John, and then a strange look came over his face. He had felt something peculiar at the bottom of one of his pockets. He pulled it out – and there was the ring!

'Goodness!' he said in astonishment. 'The merman must have slipped it into my pocket when I was in front of him on the white horse! Look, Ella! Here's your ring – now I expect you'll believe me, won't you!'

Ella took the ring with a cry of delight, and slipped it on her finger. 'I shall have to believe you!' she said. 'You really are a dear to find it for me!'

Then off they went together, and John spent the rest of the day telling Ella all about his exciting adventures with his new friends under the sea.

In the Heart
of the Wood

In the Heart of the Wood

'SCAMP! SCAMP! Do you want to go for a walk?' shouted Billy. 'Sally, are you coming too?'

A black Scottie dog flung himself on Billy and darted around in delight, his tail wagging hard. A walk! That was just what he loved!

Billy's sister came running downstairs. 'Yes, I'm coming, Billy. Let's go to the wood and watch Scamp chasing the rabbits. They all have such fun. The rabbits know he can't catch them, but Scamp always hopes he will!'

So off went the three of them to the wood. Scamp tore in front, for he had heard the magic word 'rabbits'.

Ah, one day he would catch one, he felt certain of it.

They came to the wood. It was a nice wood, but so deep and dark in the middle that the children had never walked right into the heart of it.

'Woof!' said Scamp, spying a rabbit cocking an ear at him behind a tree, and off he went. The rabbit tore off too, its white bobtail going up and down.

It went into a hole. 'Scamp always thinks that's unfair!' said Sally, with a laugh. Scamp looked up at her. He thought that rabbits should live in holes that were big enough for dogs to get down!

Another rabbit flashed by. Off went Scamp, and this time he disappeared behind the trees. The children walked on after him. They walked for some time, and didn't see Scamp at all.

'We'll have to turn back soon,' said Billy. 'Scamp! Scamp! Come along now. Home, boy, home!'

Sally whistled. No Scamp came. Bother! Now they would have to look for him.

Into the wood they went, and then heard, in the

distance, Scamp's excited barks. But he took no notice of their calls. They hurried towards him, going deeper into the wood than ever before.

Scamp was chasing a rabbit round a tree – or was the rabbit chasing him? Sally laughed. The rabbit suddenly darted off, ran to the right, and disappeared at the foot of another tree.

But what a tree! The children stared in wonder at it. They had never seen a tree so big before. Scamp ran to it and sniffed about at the bottom, where there was a hole into which the rabbit had gone.

'Let's go and look at that enormous tree,' said Sally. 'My goodness – what a size it is round the trunk!'

Billy hit it hard, and then looked at Sally, his eyes shining. 'It's hollow!' he said. 'Let's climb up and look down into the hollow. Come on!'

So into the branches of the big tree they went, up and up. Then they looked down into the hollow. The heart of the trunk was empty and rotten – completely hollow. It was a wonder that the tree was still alive!

'Let's get down into the hollow, Sally,' said Billy. 'Do let's!'

Sally looked down into the tree. 'But, Billy,' she said, 'suppose we dropped down into the hollow and couldn't climb up again. We'd have to stay there for ever and ever. Nobody would hear our calls, you know.'

'We'd better get a rope,' said Billy, peering down into the vast empty heart of the tree. 'Come on. Let's go back and get it now. I feel excited! Why, the inside of that tree is almost big enough to play house in!'

They climbed down again and rushed home, Scamp following them. He felt rather pleased with himself, because it was he who had shown them the tree they thought so wonderful!

They found a long, strong rope in the garden shed, and went off with it again. Their mother called them back.

'You can't go off now,' she said. 'It's teatime.'

'Oh well, we'll have tea and go afterwards,' said

Billy, who simply couldn't give up the idea of getting down into the hollow tree as soon as possible.

So after tea off they went. Billy had the rope tied round his waist. Scamp tore along in front, looking out for rabbits again.

'Here's the tree – gosh, it really is enormous!' said Billy, and he undid the rope round his waist. 'Come on, Sally. Up the tree we go.'

And up they went. They came to a good strong branch and Billy tied the rope firmly to it. Then he dropped the end down the middle of the tree. It fell into the dark hollow below.

'I wish we had a torch,' said Sally, peering down. 'There might be a rat down there, and I don't like rats.'

'I've brought a torch, and there won't be rats,' said Billy. 'Anyway, Scamp will soon send them away if there are.'

'You go first, Billy,' said Sally. He swung himself down on the rope – down and down, hand over hand, his legs twisting together round the rope.

He dropped with a thud into the hollow of the tree. It smelt musty. 'Come on, Sally,' he yelled, feeling for his torch. 'My word, it's like a small room inside this tree. It's most exciting.'

Sally slid down the rope. She went too fast and her hands felt as if they were burning. She landed beside Billy, on to something soft. She wondered what it was.

'Do switch on your torch,' she said. 'Quick!'

Billy switched it on – and the light shone around them in the curious tree hollow. And then they noticed something very strange.

'Look,' said Billy, puzzled, 'what's that piled here and there? Sacks! Empty sacks! And look, here's an empty cardboard box! Sally, whatever are they doing here?'

'Somebody has been using this tree for something!' said Sally. 'Oh, Billy, whose tree is it? We'd better find out!'

'You know, Sally, I think someone is using this

hollow tree to hide things in,' said Billy. 'Maybe a robber!'

'Gracious!' said Sally, scared. 'Do you mean – a burglar, perhaps? There have been an awful lot of robberies lately, haven't there? And the police have never found any of the stolen goods.'

'I say, I hope whoever uses this tree as a hiding place doesn't come while we're here,' said Billy, suddenly feeling uncomfortable.

'Well, Scamp is outside the tree. I can hear him snuffling round,' said Sally. 'He'd scare away any robbers!'

Scamp was scraping hard at a hole at the bottom of the hollow tree. Billy flashed his torch downwards and laughed. 'Look – he's got his head inside the tree but he can't get his body through. Poor old Scamp! Mind you don't get stuck!'

'Let's look at these sacks and see if they tell us anything,' said Sally. 'There are so many of them – all empty too!'

'Wait a bit – here's one with something in!' said Billy, and he picked it up. He opened the neck of the sack and flashed his torch inside.

'Sally, look – what's gleaming inside there?' he said. 'Pull it out.'

Sally put in her hand and tugged. Out came a beautiful silver candlestick, with branching ends for candles. 'Well!' said Sally. 'Look at that! This *is* a hiding place for stolen goods!'

Scamp suddenly took his head out from the hole in the tree and began to bark loudly. Sally felt frightened.

'Billy! Scamp's barking,' she said. 'Do you think someone is coming? Oh, I do hope it isn't the robbers!'

Scamp was barking his head off. 'Woof, woof, woof! Woof, woof, woof! Grrrrr!'

'Look at that dog!' said a man's hoarse voice. 'What's he doing there? Do you think there's anyone about in the woods this evening, Jim?'

'Might be,' said another voice, rather low. 'Dump the sack in that bush over there, Alf – where it won't be seen. Then we'll sit down with our backs to the hollow tree and wait a bit to see if the owner of the dog comes along. Maybe the dog's just rabbiting by himself.'

Sally clutched Billy's hand as they heard this. Men with another sack! It must be the robbers! What would they say when they found two children inside the tree!

'Shh!' said Billy, in Sally's ear. 'Don't make a sound, Sally. Perhaps Scamp will send them off. Hear how he's barking.'

The two men sat down with their backs against the tree. The children sat on the sacks, absolutely still. Scamp went on barking.

'He's just rabbiting,' said one of the men at last. 'Chuck a stone at him, Alf, and send him off!'

There was a piteous squeal from Scamp as a large stone struck him. Then the sound of scampering feet. 'He's gone,' said Alf. 'Now to get to work!'

The two men got up. Billy felt Sally trembling.

How he wished their dog Scamp had not run away. Poor Scamp – he might have been badly hurt by the stone the man threw at him.

The men began to climb up the tree. The children could hear them quite plainly. Then one of them found the rope that Billy had tied to a branch, so that he and Sally could get down easily.

'Hey, look at this!' said one of the men. 'Someone's been here! Our hiding place has been found. Someone's been down in this hollow tree.'

'Did we leave anything there in the sacks?' asked the other man. 'Yes, we did – that silver candlestick we couldn't sell! Wonder if it was found. Alf, maybe a watch is being kept on this tree!'

'Yes, better get the candlestick quick and go,' said Alf, and he slithered down the rope!

He landed right on top of poor Billy. The boy gave a yell, and the man jumped in alarm.

'What's up?' called down the other man.

'Two kids here!' answered Alf, and he gave the

children such a look that they shivered. 'Two silly, stupid, interfering kids! What are we going to do with them?'

'Ask them what they know,' called down Jim. 'Maybe no one else knows of this tree but them.'

'We only found it a little while ago,' began Sally in a trembling voice. 'Nobody else knows anything about it. Please let us go.'

The men were very angry to think that their hiding place had been found. Alf went up the tree and talked to Jim for a long time. Then he called to the children.

'Look out down there! There's a sack coming. Mind your heads!'

Billy pushed Sally aside. A sack came down and landed with a thud.

The children were astonished. Were the men going to go on using the tree then?

'We're coming back at midnight to fetch the things,' called down Alf. 'And you're going to stay down there in the tree, see, so that you can't go and tell anyone. If you're good children, maybe we'll let you out then – if you're not, we'll leave you down in the hollow!'

Sally gave a squeal. 'Oh, don't leave us here now. It's getting dark. Do let us go home. We won't say a word.'

The men pulled up the rope that hung down into the hollow. Without that to help them up the children could not possibly get out of the tree. Whatever were they to do?

The men slithered down the tree and jumped to the ground. The children heard them going through the wood. Sally was very frightened.

'Oh, Billy, can't we get out? Will we have to stay here till midnight? What will Mummy say?'

'Cheer up. We'll have to stay,' said Billy. 'Curl up on the sacks, Sally. I'll look after you. I expect they'll set us free at midnight!'

The two children settled down on the sacks inside the tree. It was very dark now. Billy felt worried. He had always been taught to look after his sister, and he didn't know how to put things right. How could they escape from the hollow tree when their rope was gone? It was quite impossible.

The children sat there in silence. Billy switched his torch on at times, just to cheer them up. He didn't like to leave it on all the time in case the battery wore out. He put his arm round Sally.

'Never mind, Sal,' he said. 'It's an adventure, you know!'

'Well, I don't like it,' said Sally. 'Oh, Billy, I hope those men really will come back. Suppose they left us here for ever?'

'Silly!' said Billy. 'Of course they wouldn't.' But all the same he felt very anxious too.

Suddenly there was a rustling sound outside the tree. Sally clutched at Billy's hand in fright. Whatever was it now? A robber creeping back? A rat? Oh dear!

'Scamp! It's old Scamp! Dear old dog, he's come back to find us!'

'Woof,' said Scamp cautiously, and stuck his head

through the hole at the bottom of the tree. He couldn't get any further. He blinked up at them.

'Scamp, can't you rescue us?' said Billy. 'No, I don't see how you can. Look at that place on his head, Sally – that must have been where the robber's stone hit him.'

'Poor old boy,' said Sally.

Suddenly Billy gave a cry and made Sally jump. 'Sally, Sally, I know what we can do! We can write a note, and tie it to Scamp's collar, and send him home with it! Can't we?'

'Oh yes,' said Sally joyfully. 'Of course. Have you got a bit of paper, Billy? I've got a pencil.'

Billy wrote on the paper:

Mother, we are prisoners in a hollow tree in the wood. It's a hiding place for stolen goods. The robbers came while we were in the tree and they have taken our rope so that we can't get out. They are coming back at midnight to get their goods. Please rescue us.

Scamp will show you where we are, if you follow him.
Love from Billy and Sally

'Mother will be surprised to get a note like that,' said Billy, and tied it firmly to Scamp's collar. He pushed it round so it stood up plainly. Then he rubbed Scamp's nose. 'Home, old boy,' he said. 'You go home with that note and find Mother. Home, old boy!'

Scamp was a clever dog. He understood. He pulled his head from the hole and backed away. Then the children heard his feet pattering through the wood.

'He's gone. Now we'll have to hope Mother sees the note and does something to save us,' said Billy. 'Cheer up, Sally. Things don't look so black after all!'

The wood was very dark and quiet, except when an owl hooted, or some small animal rustled here and there. The children sat and waited in silence, hidden deep inside the old hollow tree.

Billy looked at his watch.

'Oh dear – it's half past eleven already,' he said.

'I wonder if Mother has found the note on Scamp's collar. Surely she would have been here by now if she had.'

'Sh! I can hear something!' whispered Sally. 'Oh, it's Scamp again, surely! And somebody with him!'

It was! The children heard his eager snuffling and then many footsteps. Quite a lot of people seemed to be following Scamp.

'Here's the tree,' said their father's voice. 'What an enormous one! Billy, Sally, are you there?'

'Oh yes, Father!' cried both the children. 'We're still here. We thought you were never coming. Is Mother there?'

'Yes,' said their mother's anxious voice. 'I've been so worried about you. Listen, we told the police about your note and they are here too, planning to catch the robbers. Have they been back again?'

'Not yet. They said midnight,' said Billy. 'Is that the police we can hear all around?'

'Yes,' said a deep voice. 'This is Inspector Jenks.

We're going to get you out of that tree first, both of you. Then we're going to hide in the bushes around and completely surround the tree, to wait for the men to come back. We've got rope to haul you up. But we'll have to be quick about it!'

Someone climbed the tree, and soon after a rope came slithering down into the hollow. The children climbed out thankfully, dropped down the tree and ran to their parents. Scamp ran round and round, jumping up and down, he was so pleased to have them again!

'Now, you'd better get into the bushes too,' said the inspector. 'There's no time to take you back home. Not another sound please! Hold the dog, one of you children.'

Then there was silence, while everybody waited. Scamp began to whine softly. That meant that someone was coming. Billy quietened him. 'There's someone coming,' he whispered to the inspector, who was close by him.

So there was! It was the two robbers coming back

through the wood to the enormous hollow tree. They didn't know anyone was lying in wait. They didn't even lower their voices as they came!

They climbed the tree. They called down to the children who they thought were still in the tree. There was no answer, of course. Then down they jumped into the hollow – to find no one there!

The rest was easy. The police moved up and the tree was surrounded. The burglars were caught, their goods taken from them, and they were marched away to the police station!

'Oh, wasn't it exciting!' said Billy, as he and Sally and Scamp went home with their parents. 'I did love it!'

'Too exciting!' said his mother. 'Don't do that sort of thing too often, Billy.'

That wasn't quite the end of the story. The police sent Billy and Sally a lovely watch each for their help in catching the robbers – and Scamp had a beautiful blue collar with his name on it.

But he did deserve it, didn't he?

A Cat in Fairyland

A Cat in Fairyland

BIMBO WAS a big black cat, the finest puss in the town. His whiskers were four inches long, his tail was fat and furry. His coat shone like silk, and his purr was so loud that it sounded like a motorbike out in the road!

He belonged to Jenny and Simon, and they loved him very much.

'He is the most beautiful puss I've ever seen,' said Jenny.

'If only he could talk, it would be lovely,' said Simon. 'He's so clever he could teach us a lot.'

Bimbo often used to go out for walks with Jenny and Simon. When they took their picnic to Hallo

Wood, Bimbo ran behind them, sat down with them and shared their milk. Then he would go prowling off by himself, not very far away, always keeping the children well in sight.

One day all three started off, their picnic in a basket. They went right to the middle of Hallo Wood, sat down and began to eat. When they had finished Bimbo stalked off on his own, as usual. And suddenly a very strange thing happened.

Jenny looked up from the book she was reading and saw a strange little man, rather like a gnome, walking quietly through the trees. On his back he carried a large empty sack. Jenny nudged Simon and both children stared at the gnome in surprise and excitement, for they had never seen any kind of fairy before.

Bimbo didn't see the gnome, he was sitting down, washing himself, purring very loudly. The gnome crept up behind him, opened his large sack and suddenly flung it right over Bimbo.

Jenny and Simon jumped up at once, shouting angrily. The gnome turned and saw them. He pulled the mouth of the bag tight, threw it over his shoulder with poor Bimbo struggling inside and ran off through the wood. Jenny and Simon followed, fearful and raging, wondering what the gnome wanted with their beautiful cat.

Panting and puffing, the gnome tore through the wood, with Jenny and Simon after him. He ran into a thick bush, and when the children came up he had disappeared. They couldn't see him anywhere.

'Oh, poor Bimbo!' said Jenny, almost crying. 'Where has he been taken? Oh, Simon, we really must find him and rescue him.'

'Well, I don't see where the gnome has gone,' said Simon, puzzled. He looked round and ran here and there, but there was no sign of the gnome.

'We'd better go home and tell Mummy,' he said. 'Come on.'

But they had lost their way! They couldn't find the

path they had taken in following the gnome, and they were quite lost. Jenny began to feel frightened, and wondered if the gnome would come back and take them prisoner too, but Simon cheered her up, and said that he would fight a dozen gnomes if he could see them.

'There's a little path running along here,' he said to Jenny. 'We'd better follow it. It must lead somewhere.'

So they ran down it, and after some time they came to the prettiest little cottage they had ever seen, so small that it really didn't look much more than a large doll's house.

Simon knocked at the yellow front door, and a pixie with silvery wings opened it. She looked so surprised to see them.

'We've lost our way,' said Simon politely. 'Could you please help us?'

'Come in,' said the pixie. 'Mind your heads.'

They had to stoop down to go inside, for the door was so small. Inside the cottage were small chairs and a tiny table. It was the funniest little place. Jenny was half afraid of sitting down in case she broke the chair she sat on.

'Let me offer you a cup of tea,' said the pixie, and she hurried to her small fireplace and took a boiling kettle off the hob.

'Well, we've already had tea,' said Simon, 'but it would be nice to have a cup of pixie tea, so thank you very much, we will.'

Then, while the pixie made sweet-smelling tea in a little flowery teapot, and set out tiny currant cakes, Simon and Jenny told her all about the gnome who had stolen Bimbo, their cat.

'Now did you ever hear such a thing!' said the pixie in surprise. 'I'm sure I know where your puss has been taken.'

'Oh, where?' asked the children at once.

'To the old wizard, Too-Tall,' said the pixie, handing the plate of cakes to Jenny. 'I know that his last cat, who used to help him in his spells, ran away a little while ago, and he has been wanting another. That gnome you saw is his servant, and I expect he has been looking out for a good black cat. When he saw your Bimbo he captured him at once, and I expect he took him straight to his master, Too-Tall.'

'But Bimbo would hate to help anyone with spells,' said Jenny. 'He's just an ordinary cat, and he would be very unhappy to live away from us. The wizard has no right to take him!'

'Could we rescue him, do you think?' asked Simon. 'Where does this wizard live?'

'He lives in Runaway House, not very far from here,' said the pixie.

'What a funny name!' said the children.

'Well, it's a funny house,' said the pixie. 'It's got four little legs underneath it, and when the wizard wants to move, he just tells it to run where he wants it to, and the legs run away at once, taking the house with them.'

'Gracious!' said Jenny, her eyes shining with

excitement. 'Wouldn't I like to see it!'

'I'll take you there, if you like,' said the pixie, and she wrapped a little coat round her. 'But mind – don't make a noise when we get there, or the old wizard might put a spell on us.'

'Will we be able to rescue Bimbo, do you think?' asked Simon.

'We'll see when we get there,' said the pixie, opening the front door. 'Come along.'

She took them back to the thick bush where the gnome had disappeared. To the children's surprise they saw a little trapdoor hidden under the bush. The pixie pulled it open, and all three of them climbed down some steps into an underground passage. Then for some way they walked in darkness, guided only by the pixie's voice in front of them. Soon a little lamp shone out, and Jenny and Simon saw a lot of doors in front of them.

The pixie opened a blue one and led the way into a small room, where a grey rabbit was writing at a desk.

He looked up, and asked where they wanted to go.

'To Runaway House,' answered the pixie. The rabbit gave them each a little green ticket, and told them to sit on three small toadstools in the corner. They all sat down and the rabbit pressed a button. In a second the three toadstools shot upwards and Jenny and Simon clutched at the edges in surprise.

For a long time they went up and up, but at last the toadstools slowed down. They came to a stop inside another small room where a second rabbit sat. He took their tickets, opened a door and showed them out into the sunshine.

'What an adventure!' said Simon, who was thoroughly enjoying himself. 'I did like riding on those toadstools!'

They were on a hillside, and the pixie pointed to a little house at the top, surrounded on three sides by trees, to shelter it from the wind.

'That's Runaway House,' she said. 'You can see the feet peeping from underneath it. When it runs, it raises itself on its legs and goes off like lightning!'

The three made their way up to it, and the pixie tiptoed to a little window at the back. She peeped inside, and beckoned to the children. They crept up and looked in.

Bimbo was inside! He sat on the floor in the middle of a chalk ring, looking very angry and very miserable. His great tail swept the floor from side to side and his fine whiskers twitched angrily.

The wizard Too-Tall, a thin, bent old man in a pointed hat, was standing opposite the cat, waving a long stick. He looked very cross. In a corner by the fireplace, stirring something in a big pot, was the gnome who had stolen Bimbo.

'You must help me with my magic spells, or I will turn you into a mouse!' said the wizard to Bimbo. And then to the children's enormous surprise, Bimbo opened his mouth and spoke.

'Are your spells all good ones?' he asked. 'For I tell you this, Master Wizard, no cat belonging to my honourable family would ever help in making a bad spell for witches or goblins to use!'

'I am not a good wizard,' said Too-Tall with a horrid smile. 'I make my money by selling magic to witches, and if you are too grand to help me, my honourable cat, I shall have to do as I said, and turn you into a mouse. Then you will be hunted by your honourable family, and be punished for your stupidity.'

Poor Bimbo began to tremble, but he still would not agree to help Too-Tall, and the wizard grew impatient.

'I will give you one more chance,' he said at last. 'Unless you stand up on your hind legs, turn round twice and mew seven times loudly while I chant my magic words and wave my enchanted stick, you shall be changed into a little brown mouse!'

He began to wave his long stick and chant curious words, which made the little pixie outside shiver and shake. But Bimbo did not stand up and mew as he had been told. He sat there in the middle of the ring, looking very much frightened, but quite determined not to help the wicked old wizard.

Then Too-Tall lost his patience. He struck Bimbo with his stick, called out a magic word and then laughed loudly – for the black cat suddenly vanished, and in his place cowered a tiny brown mouse.

'Now you see what your punishment is!' cried the wizard. 'Go, hide yourself away, miserable creature, and be sure that when I get another cat you will be hunted for your life!'

The little mouse rushed away into a corner, and hid itself in an old slipper. Jenny and Simon could hardly believe their eyes when they saw that their lovely Bimbo had vanished, and in his place was a poor little mouse. Jenny began to cry, but Simon doubled up his fists, half inclined to go in and fight the wizard and gnome.

'Don't do anything foolish,' whispered the pixie, dragging the two away from the window. 'Hush, Jenny, don't cry, or the wizard will hear you and he might quite easily change all of us into mice too.'

'But I must do something about poor Bimbo,' said Simon fiercely.

'Well, I've got a plan,' said the pixie. 'Listen. We'll wait until darkness comes, and then borrow three spades from Tippy, an elf who lives nearby. We'll dig a big hole just a little way down the hill. Then we'll all borrow trays and trumpets, and make a fearful noise outside the house. The wizard will wake in a fright and think a great army is marching against him. He will order his house to run away, and as the only way it can run is down the hill because there are trees on every other side, it will fall straight into the pit we have dug for it.'

'What then?' asked the children in excitement, thinking it was a marvellous plan.

'Well, I'll pop inside the house before the wizard has got over his fright, and get his enchanted stick,' said the pixie delightedly. 'He's no good without that, you know. You, Simon, must get hold of the gnome and hold him tightly. You, Jenny, must pick up the little mouse. The wizard will probably run away, for he is an awful coward without his magic stick!'

'Go on, go on!' cried the children, their eyes shining.

'That's all,' said the pixie. 'We'll just run off to Tippy's then, and I'll see what I can do about Bimbo for you.'

Night was coming on, for the sun had gone down over the hill. The pixie led the way to a large toadstool on the other side of the hill. It had a little door in it and the pixie knocked. An elf opened the door, and peeped out.

'Who is it?' he asked.

'It's only Tuffy the pixie,' said the pixie. 'Can you lend us three spades, Tippy?'

'Certainly,' said Tippy, and he took three little spades from a corner of his strange toadstool house. The pixie took them, said thank you and ran off again with the children. They passed the wizard's house, which was now lit inside by a swinging lamp, and went a little way down the hillside.

Then they began to dig. How they dug! The pixie said a spell over their spades to make them work quickly, and the hole soon began to grow. The spades flew in and out, and the children got quite out of breath.

At last it was finished. The moon shone out in the sky, and the pixie said they had better wait for a big cloud to come before they carried out the next part of their plan, for if the house could see before it as it ran, it would run round the hole they had made, instead of into it.

'I'll take the spades back to Tippy's and borrow a few trays and things,' whispered the pixie. 'You stay here, and watch to see that everything is all right.'

It wasn't long before the pixie was back again. She had with her three trays, two trumpets and a large whistle. She giggled as she handed out the things to the children.

'What a shock the wizard will get!' she said. 'Now

creep with me just outside the cottage, and when I say, "Go!" bang on your trays and blow your trumpets hard. I'll blow my whistle, and if we don't give the wizard the fright of his life, I shall be surprised!'

They all crept up to the cottage. 'Go!' shouted the pixie suddenly, as soon as a cloud came over the moon. In a second there was a most fearful noise! The trays clanged, the trumpets blared, the whistle blew and, in between, all three shouted at the tops of their voices.

The wizard was sitting at his table eating his supper with the gnome. When they heard the fearful din outside the wizard leapt to his feet and turned very pale.

'It's the elfin army after us!' he shouted. 'House, house, find your feet, run away, fast and fleet!'

At once the house stood up on its four legs and began to move. It raced down the hill, straight towards the big hole that the children and the pixie had dug.

Plonk! It fell right into it. Chimneys flew about, windows smashed and the wizard and the gnome cried out in terror. They couldn't get out of the door because it was buried in the pit, so they tried to get out of the window.

'Come on!' cried the pixie. 'Into the house, all of you!'

Jenny and Simon rushed to the fallen house. They climbed in at one window, and the pixie climbed in at another. Jenny ran to the corner where she saw the frightened little mouse peeping out of a slipper. She picked it up and slipped it into her pocket.

Simon rushed at the gnome and held him tightly, then called to Jenny to tie him up with a piece of rope he saw lying by the fire. The pixie snatched up the wizard's enchanted stick with a cry of delight.

The old wizard had scrambled out of his window and was rushing down the hill in the moonlight. He was frightened out of his wits!

'Leave the gnome and come away now,' said the pixie. 'If that old wizard meets any witch he knows, he may bring her back here, and that would be awkward.'

The three climbed out of the tumbled-down house and ran down the hillside to give back the trays, trumpets and whistle. As they came back again the pixie pointed to the east with a shout of dismay.

'There's the wizard with two witches! Come on, we shall have to hurry.'

She took the children to the door that led to the toadstool room where the rabbit sat. In a flash they had their tickets and were sitting on three toadstools. Just as the strange lifts had started to rush downwards the wizard and witches came racing into the room, and sat down on other toadstools.

'Ooh, my, now we're in for a race!' groaned the pixie. 'Jump off your toadstools as soon as they stop and run for the door. Race down the passage and up the steps to the trapdoor as fast as you can!'

So as soon as the toadstools stopped, Jenny and Simon leapt off them, ran to the door and raced into the passage as fast as their legs would carry them. The pixie followed, and even as they all reached the door they saw the wizard and witches landing in the room on their toadstools.

They tore along the passage and up the steps, with the wizard and witches after them. When they got outside they banged the trapdoor down, but the wizard pushed it open almost at once. Then the pixie gave a shout of triumph.

'What a silly I am! I'd forgotten about Too-Tall's enchanted stick!' she cried. 'I'll soon settle him!'

She waited until Too-Tall and the witches had climbed out of the trapdoor, and then she danced towards them, waving the stick and chanting a long string of words.

The wizard gave a howl of fright, and raced back to the trapdoor. The witches followed, and soon there was a bang as the trapdoor closed.

'They're gone, and they won't come back in a hurry!' said the pixie in delight. 'What a good thing I remembered I had Too-Tall's stick. I can use it on Bimbo too, and change him back to a cat.'

They all hurried to the pixie's cottage. She drew a circle of chalk on the floor, put the frightened mouse in the middle, waved the enchanted stick and cried out a magic word. Immediately the mouse vanished, and in its place appeared Bimbo, the big black cat!

Bimbo gave a loud purr and leapt over to the delighted children. What a fuss he made of them! They stroked him and loved him and he rubbed his big head against them.

'Now what about a hot cup of cocoa and a slice of cake?' asked the pixie. 'It's quite time you went home, you know, or your mother will be very worried about you.'

So they all sat down to hot cocoa and slices of ginger cake. Then the pixie showed them the way home through the wood. She shook hands with them, stroked Bimbo and said goodbye.

'Goodbye,' said Jenny and Simon, 'and thank you ever so much for helping us. We only wish we could do something in return for your kindness.'

'Don't forget I've got the wizard's magic stick!' said the little pixie with a laugh. 'I never in all my life expected to have such a wonderful thing as that! That's quite enough reward for me! Now goodbye to you both, and run home quickly.'

Off went Jenny, Simon and Bimbo, and very soon they ran up the path to their house. Their mother was looking for them, and was getting very anxious. When she heard their story she looked most astonished.

'What an extraordinary thing!' she cried. 'I can hardly believe it, my dears.'

'Well, Mummy, we'll get Bimbo to guide us to the pixie's cottage in Hallo Wood tomorrow,' said Jenny.

So the next day they told Bimbo to take them there – but wasn't it a pity, he couldn't remember the way!

'Perhaps he will one day,' said Simon. 'We must wait for that.'

And as far as I know, they are still waiting.

Mr Pippin's
Lemonade

Mr Pippin's Lemonade

IT WAS a very hot day and Mr Pippin was fast asleep in the garden when his wife woke him up.

'Pippin, Pippin!' she called. 'Where are you? I've made some lovely lemonade, and I want you to take it to the market and sell it all to the passersby for tenpence a cup. It is such a hot day that folks will buy a lot, and then we shall have a chance to make ourselves some money.'

Mr Pippin didn't want to walk to the market on a hot day one little bit. But he knew he would have to, so he got up, and took the big can of lemonade from his wife. She gave him a lot of little cups, and ran a string through their handles so that he would be able to carry them all easily over his shoulder. Off he went to the market.

Now on the way he tasted the lemonade, and he thought it was very good.

'My!' said Mr Pippin. 'That really is splendid lemonade, I shall easily sell the lot. I should think there is quite enough in the can to fill forty cups. That means forty tenpence pieces, which is four pounds. Ha! That's a lot of money!'

Mr Pippin became really quite excited.

'If I had four pounds I would be able to buy some of Mrs Biscuit's buns, which are only fivepence each, put some jam in the middle and then sell them for tenpence each,' he said to himself, walking along just as fast as he could.

'Oooh! Eighty buns would put eight pounds into my pocket. I should buy a hen to lay eggs. The eggs would hatch out into chicks, and I could sell them all. I should soon have quite enough money to buy myself a goat.'

He was so excited at the thought of having a goat of his own that he stopped quite still.

'A goat. Why, I could sell its milk and make a great deal of money – enough to buy a sheep perhaps. Think of having a nice woolly sheep. It could feed in the field behind my cottage, and each year it would give me plenty of wool. Soon I should get enough money from my wool to buy a horse. That could live in the field too. I would let the farmers borrow it for ten pounds a day. They would be sure to pay that much for a good horse like mine. How rich I should be.'

On and on he walked, and soon he could see the market in the distance. He was glad, because his can of lemonade was getting very heavy.

'When I am rich I will never, ever walk to market again,' he said. 'I will ride in my carriage and I shall get a brand-new coat for myself and a new hat.'

He was so pleased that he skipped a few steps, and

some of the lemonade in the can flew out, splashing away into the road.

'I shall buy a fine new cottage too,' he said. 'My own is so damp, and it has only two small rooms. Oh, shan't I be grand! I shall walk with my head held high in the air, and I shall order everyone about and tell them just what to do.'

Mr Pippin felt so grand that he didn't look where he was going, and he very nearly fell into the ditch. That frightened him, and he walked slowly to the market, looking carefully where he was going, in case he should spill any more of his lemonade.

At last he got to the market, and he sat down on the kerb, by his can of lemonade. He was so excited with thinking of all the grand plans he had made that his cheeks were as red as fire and his eyes were shining bright.

'You look very, very happy today, Pippin!' said Mrs String, the farmer's wife. 'Have you found some money somewhere or something like that?'

'No,' said Mr Pippin, 'I'm going to be very rich, that's why I'm happy.'

'How are you going to be rich?' asked Mrs String, who didn't believe that a lazy fellow like Pippin would ever earn any money.

'Well, I shall sell this lemonade, and with it I shall buy some of Mrs Biscuit's buns, which I'll sell for tenpence each, with jam in,' said Mr Pippin, excited. 'Then I'll buy a hen who can lay me some eggs, and when they hatch out I'll sell them and buy a goat. Oh! I'll soon be rich.'

Dame Wimple and Farmer Slap came up to hear Mr Pippin talking. They smiled when they heard him talking about being rich.

'Ho! You may well smile,' cried Mr Pippin. 'I shall sell my goat's milk and buy a sheep and sell its wool and buy a horse. And I'll hire out my horse to you, Farmer Slap, for ten pounds a day.'

'I shouldn't pay you one pound!' said Farmer Slap, and he laughed. 'You won't get rich, Pippin.'

'I will, I will!' cried Mr Pippin, and he grew red in the face again. 'Oh, I'll be very grand indeed. I'll buy a new coat and a new hat, and a carriage to drive about in. And I'll buy a new cottage, and I'll buy a great big dog.'

'Whatever for?' asked Farmer Slap.

'To set loose when you come to see me,' cried Mr Pippin angrily. 'Yes, that will make you frightened all right! I'll turn him loose as soon as you get inside my gate, and he will rush at you barking as loudly as he can. And you'll run away and try your best to dodge him, like this.'

Mr Pippin pretended that a dog was after him, and he dodged from side to side, pretending to be very much frightened.

But, alas, he didn't look where he was going, and he stepped right into his can of lemonade! Over it went and Mr Pippin went with it! He was completely soaked in the sticky lemonade, and a very sorry sight he looked when he sat up.

'Oh, oh!' he groaned. 'There goes my lemonade – and my buns – and my hen and eggs – and my goat – and my sheep – and my horse – and my new coat and hat – and my carriage. Boo-hoo-hoo-hoo!'

'You shouldn't have been so spiteful as to set your imaginary dog on me!' said Farmer Slap, laughing. 'It serves you right!'

Poor Mr Pippin! I feel quite sorry for him, don't you?

The Jackdaw
Afternoon

The Jackdaw Afternoon

THE FOUR boys were out on a bike ride together – Bill, Peter, Bob and Martin. They had their lunch with them in paper bags, and were looking for a place to sit down and eat their sandwiches.

'Look – let's go to that old tumbledown tower!' said Bill. 'See – over there, where those big birds are flying round and round.'

'They're jackdaws,' said Bob. 'They must be nesting in the old tower. Jackdaws like to nest in places like that.'

'How do they build their nests there?' asked Bill. 'I should have thought that twigs would keep falling down the tower!'

'They do,' said Bob. 'But as they bring quite long ones some of them stick in the tower – and then other twigs fall against them and soon big, clumsy nests are built. I bet jackdaws have been nesting over there for years!'

They rode to the old ruined tower. Broken-down walls ran here and there, and round about the tower lay sticks that the jackdaws had dropped before they had reached their nesting place.

'What a row they make!' said Martin, leaning his bicycle against an old wall. 'Chack-chack-chack! Is that why they're called chackdaws!'

'Probably!' said Bob, who knew a lot about birds. 'Look at them circling about in the air. I wonder which one is their leader?'

'Who cares?' said Peter. 'I'm more interested in lunch than birds. Come on – here's a good place. I'm ravenous!'

They all sat down and began their lunch. A big jackdaw looked down at them from a nearby wall.

'Chack!' he said. 'Chack-chack!'

'He's not saying, "chack!" He's saying, "chuck!"' said Peter. 'He wants us to chuck him a piece of bread. Here you are, jackdaw!' He threw a piece of bread towards the big black bird. It at once flew down to it, and was immediately followed by about a dozen others.

'Hey, get away – the bread belongs to the first fellow!' shouted Pete, and he picked up a stone and threw it at the excited birds. They rose into the air at once.

'Stop that,' said Bob angrily. 'Stoning birds is a coward's trick.'

'Farmers shoot rooks, don't they?' said Martin sulkily. 'I bet jackdaws are as much of a pest as rooks are.'

'Well, they're not – and, if they were, stoning them isn't a decent way to get rid of them,' said Bob. 'It only lames them or breaks a wing.'

The jackdaws flew down again. Martin picked up another stone and so did Bill, grinning at Bob's angry face.

'Shut up, you two,' said Pete, munching sandwiches. 'You know what Bob is about birds – he's cracked on them. Don't let's start quarrelling, for pity's sake.'

Martin and Bill dropped their stones. Bob threw no more bits and pieces for the jackdaws, afraid that the other two boys might begin stoning them again. The birds flew around, chacking loudly, but did not come to the ground again. Bob was very thankful!

Pete handed round some chocolate, and they all lay back in the sun to eat it. Bill and Martin wanted to have some sort of game but they were too lazy to get up and play one.

'Let's set up one of our ginger beer bottles and throw stones at that, seeing that we aren't allowed to chuck stones at the dear dickybirds,' said Martin, with a laugh. 'Any objection to that, Bob? Sure we shan't frighten the bottle, or upset its nerves?'

'Don't be an ass,' said Bob. 'And you jolly well know we're not allowed to chuck stones and break bottles. The head told us the other day that fires on heaths and commons are often begun by the sun shining on bits of broken glass on the ground. Don't be idiots.'

Bill yawned. 'Doesn't seem as if we're allowed to do anything,' he said to Martin in a bored voice. 'I think I'll get up and have a wander around. I don't expect Bob will forbid us to do that, will you, Bob?'

'Oh, don't be potty!' said Bob, losing his temper. 'Just because I didn't want you to lame or wing a bird! Don't be fat-heads.'

'He's told us not to be asses, idiots, potty or fat-heads,' said Martin to Bill. 'Come on, let's go off by ourselves. I've had enough of Bob. Coming, Pete?'

'Yes, I think I will,' said Pete, getting up too. 'I shall fall asleep if I don't get up. Coming, Bob?'

'No,' said Bob, still angry. 'I'll stay here and look after the bikes.'

'Well, don't fall asleep, or you won't be able to watch your dickybirds,' said Martin and hopped out of Bob's reach, laughing. The three went off together.

Bob lazed in the sun, watching the jackdaws as they circled above his head. They went to perch on the tower, chattering together in their sociable way. Bob watched them, and thought they were very like boys hobnobbing together, telling their news to one another.

Suddenly, with loud cries, the birds rose up all together into the air, their wings making quite a noise. Bob wondered what had disturbed them. He soon knew!

He heard the sound of a stone clattering over the old, broken paving of the tower yard – and then another. Martin and Bill were throwing stones again – and perhaps Peter too! But surely not at the jackdaws again?

Bob sprang to his feet and went to find the others. They were standing at the other side of the tower, looking up at it. Martin had a big stone in his hand. He grinned when he saw Bob. 'It's all right. We're not throwing at the birds! We're trying to see who can first get a stone right into the top of the tower!'

'But you *know* the birds are nesting there,' said Bob. 'There may be young ones in the nests. You'll hit them.'

'Go on! We shan't any of us get a stone right into the top of the tower!' said Pete. 'Don't worry, Bob – we shan't hurt anything.'

Bill threw his stone right up into the air, through the circling birds. It didn't hit any of them because the birds swerved aside. It went up and up, made a curve in the air – and then dropped very neatly indeed right into the top of the old tower!

'He's done it!' shouted Martin. 'Jolly good, Bill.'

The jackdaws suddenly seemed to sense danger. They flew down low and surrounded the three boys who stood together, chacking at the tops of their harsh voices.

'They're attacking us!' shouted Martin in fright, and ran for his bicycle. The birds followed. Bill and Pete were scared too, for there suddenly seemed to be hundreds of noisy birds round them with big, strong beaks!

They leapt on their bicycles and rode off down the hillside. The jackdaws soon gave up the strange chase and flew back to the tower, talking loudly to one another.

Only Bob was left. The jackdaws had taken no notice of him at all. They knew he had thrown no stones!

Bob stared after the others. It served them right, having to go off in a hurry like that! He looked up at the tower. That big stone Bill had thrown had gone right into the tower – no doubt about that. It might have destroyed a nest or two if it had fallen into the mass of twigs that lined the crevices of the tower.

'I think I'll go in at the old door of the tower and look up it,' said Bob to himself. 'I may find the big stone too, that Bill threw. How maddening of him! Now our outing is spoilt, because the birds chased the others away.'

He went in through the old, ruined door. The

tower was rather dark inside and Bob had to get his eyes used to the dimness. Then he saw a mass of twigs on the floor, which the birds must themselves have dropped down the tower as they built their nests. He saw something else too – a young jackdaw, a nestling, lying among the twigs, its mouth opening and shutting.

Bob went over to it. He saw at once what had happened. The stone had hit a nest, and had struck the nestling inside too. The nest of twigs had been sent downwards and had broken when it reached the ground. The frightened nestling, bruised and trembling, could do nothing but lie there and wait for its parents – and they hadn't come.

Bob bent down over the small bird. It had plenty of feathers, and its eyes were bright as it looked up at him. The boy picked it up gently, and parted the feathers to see if the bird was badly hurt.

One of its wings was damaged, but otherwise it seemed all right. 'I'll take you home and look after you,' said Bob. 'I've always wanted a tame jackdaw! If I leave you here you'll die. There, now – I'll tuck you gently inside my shirt. You'll be all right, you funny little thing!'

The bird gave a tiny squawk as if to say, 'Be careful, please!' and settled down inside Bob's shirt. It felt nice there. Bob liked it.

He was just going off to his bike when something caught his eye, something that shone out from the broken nest of twigs. He stirred the fallen nest with his foot, and at once what looked like a little wriggling, glittering snake fell through the twigs on to the ground below.

'What *is* it?' said Bob, puzzled. He bent down and burrowed about in the heap of twigs. His fingers closed over something hard and he picked it up.

How amazed he was! In his hand he held a shining necklace – why, surely it must be made of diamonds, the stones glittered so brightly! He slipped it into his pocket, excited.

'Jackdaws like bright things! They take them away when they find them, and hide them in their nests, or in any odd corner. This necklace must have been seen through somebody's window by a bright-eyed jackdaw – and he flew down and took it! Goodness me – and I found it!'

He mounted his bicycle, his head in a whirl. He had a wonderful necklace in his pocket and a jackdaw down his shirt. What would the other boys say when they knew?

He went first to the police station, which was on his way home – and he was quite right, the necklace *was* made of diamonds!

'Good gracious! This was stolen three months ago!' said the sergeant. 'And we never *could* find the thief! Who stole it?'

'This chap's father, I expect!' said Bob and opened his shirt to show the astonished policeman the little bird he had inside. 'The necklace was in his nest.'

'Well, thanks a lot,' said the sergeant. 'There is a

good reward offered for this, my boy – and you'll be the one to get it!'

The reward was fifty pounds, and Bob *did* get it! He has bought presents for all his family, a model yacht for himself and a fine cage to bring up his pet jackdaw in till its wing is mended and it can fly.

As for the other boys, they could hardly believe their ears. *Fifty* pounds! A diamond necklace! Why hadn't *they* gone to make sure they hadn't hurt a young bird in that tower?

'Lucky Bob!' said Martin enviously. 'I bet he's thrilled with the fifty pounds!'

But Bob is much more thrilled with his pet jackdaw. It follows him all over the place now, sits on his shoulder and talks into his ear. It's a really amusing bird, and worth much more than the fifty pounds to Bob.

But alas! He's just missed his silver pencil! Now, wherever *can* it be? (Ask the jackdaw!)

A Real Fairy Fair

A Real Fairy Fair

'YOU'VE BOTH been good children, so you may go to the fair in the next village for a treat,' said Mother, on Whit Monday.

'Oh, Mother, how lovely!' exclaimed Mollie. 'Can we go now?'

'Yes,' answered Mother, 'and here is sixpence each for you to spend on sweets and on swings, if you like.'

'Thank you,' said Wilfrid, taking the sixpences, 'I'll take care of them. Shall we go through the wood?'

'Yes, dears. Goodbye!' cried Mother, waving to them as they went off. 'Have a good time!'

Wilfrid and Mollie ran through the fields, kicking

a ball along that they had brought with them. When they reached the wood Wilfrid picked up the ball, afraid that it would get lost in the long grass.

'Come along!' shouted Mollie, running. 'Let's hurry up and get to the fair.'

'Oh, Mollie, just look here,' called Wilfrid, stopping under a lovely pink may tree.

'What?' asked Mollie, stopping.

'Look at this glorious pink may blossom. Let's pick a bit for a buttonhole.'

'I can't reach,' said Mollie, after trying hard to pick a little bit.

'I'll throw my ball up, then perhaps it will knock a bit down,' said Wilfrid.

He threw up his ball, as hard as he could. They both watched it go up into the pink may – but it didn't come down alone. Something else came down with it. Something that wasn't pink may blossom.

'Wilfrid, oh, Wilfrid,' said Mollie, 'we've hit a *fairy*, and knocked her down.'

Sure enough it *was* a fairy. And there she lay moaning, on the grass, dressed in pink like the may, and with long wings like a dragonfly.

'Oh,' she sobbed, 'oh, you *have* hurt me. You horrid, cruel children!'

'Oh dear,' said Wilfrid, kneeling down by her. 'Do forgive us. We only tried to knock a bit of may down. We wouldn't have hit you for *anything*.'

'Well, if it was an accident, of course I'll forgive you,' said Morfael, the little may fairy. 'But what am I to do? One of my wings is hurt, and I can't fly back to Fairyland.'

'Can we help you?' asked Mollie.

'Yes, if you will. But have you got time? You would have to carry me right to the other end of the wood, and then down the oak tree passage.'

'Well, we *were* going to the fair,' said Mollie sadly, 'but as we've hurt you we'll do our best to make up for it, and we'll stay and help you.'

'Oh, Mollie,' said Wilfrid, feeling his two

sixpences, 'we shan't have any time for swings and sweets if we don't go straight along now.'

'Never mind,' said Mollie, picking up the little fairy.

Off the three went, Morfael telling Mollie exactly which way to go. It seemed a long way, and Wilfrid began to get tired.

'Are we nearly there?' he asked at last.

'Yes, here we are,' answered Morfael, as they reached a large oak tree. 'Knock on the tree seven times, Mollie, and say "akraidafarray" softly.'

Mollie did so, and a little door in the tree slid quickly open, and showed steps going down and down. Down they all went, seeing their way by the light of queer-shaped lamps hung along the passages.

At last they came out into the sunshine again among glorious flowers amid hundreds of fairies. Mollie and Wilfrid looked on in delight.

'This is Fairyland,' said Morfael, 'and here is the queen coming.'

A beautiful buttercup carriage drew up, and the queen stepped out.

'Why, Morfael, what's the matter?' she cried, seeing her broken wing.

'I've hurt my wing,' said Morfael, 'and these children carried me here out of kindness. They *were* going to the Whit-Monday Fair, but I'm afraid they won't have time now.'

'Oh, never mind,' said the queen, 'we've got a much better Whit-Monday Fair in Fairyland. Will you come to ours instead?'

'We'd *love* to,' answered the children in delight. To go to a real fairy fair was something simply glorious!

They stepped into the queen's buttercup carriage, and off they went to the fair. They had a most lovely time, and as you can do everything in Fairyland without paying, they didn't even have to spend their sixpences.

The swings were made of spider's web, strong and very soft. Mollie thought she would like to swing in one all day. There were roundabouts with real birds and bees for horses, instead of just wooden ones. And, instead of clanking music when the roundabout went round, all the birds began to sing, and that was so much nicer.

The fairies were very kind to them and took them to see all the sights, and there were certainly a great many wonderful things to see.

'Could we go on that river in one of those waterlily boats?' asked Molly.

'Well, it's getting late for you,' answered the fairies, 'so that must be the last thing you do. The boat will take you home by itself, so we'll say goodbye to you here.'

'Goodbye,' called the children, getting into the white waterlily boat, 'and thank you for giving us such a *lovely* time.'

Off floated the boat, and presently Mollie said, 'Wilfrid! This is the little stream that runs through the field by our house! And oh! Look, there's our house over there!'

Out they jumped, very surprised that their stream should flow from Fairyland. Mother was waiting for them, and could hardly believe her ears when they told her of all their adventures.

'Well,' said Wilfrid, as he got into bed that night, 'of all the fairs there have been this Whit Monday, I think our fairy fair must have been the *very best*!'

'And so do I,' said Mollie. 'I *do* hope we can go again next year!'

The Very Brave Puppy

The Very Brave Puppy

ONE DAY, when Martin and Clare were walking home from school, they saw a little puppy struggling to swim in a pond.

'Quick! Let's get it out!' cried Clare.

Martin took off his shoes and socks, waded into the pond and picked up the struggling puppy. He quickly carried the shivering little creature back to the bank.

'Let's take it home, and see if Mummy will let us keep it,' said Clare. 'Poor little thing!'

They carried the puppy home – but, oh dear, their mother wouldn't let them keep it.

'No,' she said, 'you have two rabbits and a kitten and that's quite enough. You can't have a puppy too. Besides, it is a very ugly little thing.'

'But what shall we do with it?' asked Clare.

'Your father's got to go to town this afternoon and he'll take it to the Dogs' Home,' said Mummy. 'It will be looked after there until someone comes and offers to give it a good home. You had better go into town too, and have your hair cut, both of you.'

So that afternoon Daddy and the two children got into their car and drove off to town. Clare carried the puppy, which wriggled and licked her happily, thinking it had found lovely owners at last. The children thought it was the nicest little puppy they had ever seen, and even Daddy said it wasn't a bad little thing when it had licked the back of his ear a dozen times.

'Here's the hairdresser's,' said Daddy, pulling up by the kerb. 'Come on, you two. Leave the puppy in the car, and we'll all go and have our hair cut.'

So into the shop they went, leaving the puppy in the car. Soon all three were sitting in chairs with big white cloths round them, and snip, snip, went the scissors.

Outside the shop were two men. They had seen Daddy and the children go into the hairdresser's and they knew that it would be some time before they came out again.

'Let's take this car, Bill,' said one of the men. 'We can jump into it and drive off before anyone stops us!'

'But isn't that a dog inside?' said the other man.

'Pooh, that's only a puppy!' said the first man. 'Come on, quick, before a policeman comes!'

He opened the car door and at the same moment the puppy started barking his very loudest, for he knew quite well that the two men were not the children, nor their father. The man cuffed the puppy, who bared his little white teeth and snarled. He was very much afraid of this nasty rough man, but the car was in his charge, and he was going to guard it as best he could.

So he flew at the man who was trying to sit in the driver's seat, and bit him on the arm. The man tore him away and flung him into the back of the car, but, still barking, the brave little dog once more hurled himself at the thief.

Then Martin and Clare heard him barking, and Martin ran to the window and looked out.

'Daddy, Daddy!' he cried. 'There're two men stealing the car! Quick! Quick! The puppy is trying to stop them, but they'll soon be away!'

Daddy rushed out of the shop at once, followed by the hairdresser and another man. Quickly they captured the two thieves and the hairdresser went to telephone the police. In a few minutes the bad men were marched off to the police station, and Daddy and the children went back to have their hair finished.

'Well, that puppy is about the bravest little thing I ever saw!' said Daddy. 'I've a good mind to keep him, after this. He stopped our car from being stolen, there's no doubt of that. What about taking him home again, children, and telling Mummy what he's done? Perhaps she would let you keep him then.'

'Oh, Daddy!' cried Martin and Clare in delight. 'Do let's!'

So they all drove home again and Daddy told Mummy how the puppy's bravery had saved their car from being stolen. The puppy looked at Mummy with his brown eyes, and wagged his stumpy tail hopefully.

'Well, we'll keep him!' said Mummy. 'I'm sure he will grow up into a very brave, faithful dog. You shall have him, children.'

So that is how Pickles the puppy came to belong to Martin and Clare. He is a grown-up dog now and he has scared away burglars twice and once he pulled the baby out of the water when she fell in. Mummy is very glad she let Martin and Clare keep him – and of course they think he is the very best dog in the world!

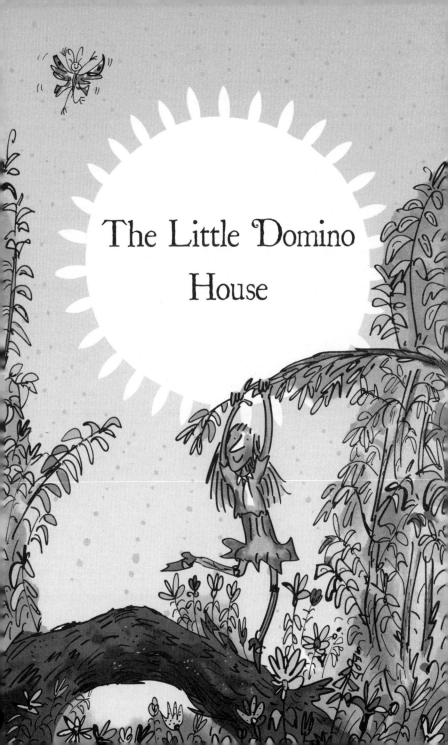

The Little Domino House

The Little Domino House

BUNTY WAS playing in the garden when she heard a funny noise. 'Where does that come from?' she wondered. 'It sounds as if it's over the wall. I'll go and see.'

She peeped over the wall, and at first could see nothing. Then, goodness me, whatever was that in the grass? Surely, surely, it couldn't be an elf!

Bunty felt her cheeks grow red with excitement. Suppose it was! She had always looked for fairies and had never seen one. It really and truly did look like one. And what a funny noise it was making – almost as if it was crying with rage!

Bunty ran to the gate in the wall and opened it. She went to the little figure in the grass and bent down to look at it closely. Yes, sure enough it was an elf, there wasn't a doubt of that. It had a pair of blue wings, and wore a pointed cap and pointed shoes.

It was stamping its feet in the grass, and crying and shouting angrily. When it saw Bunty it shook its tiny fist at her and cried, 'Was it you who took my toadstool house away?'

'Goodness, no!' said Bunty. 'I've only just this minute come here, because I heard the noise you were making. What's the matter?'

'Well,' said the elf, drying his angry tears on a buttercup petal which he used for a handkerchief, 'I grew myself a fine toadstool house, and moved all my furniture in there. The fairy queen asked me to send out all the invitations to her next dance, so I told the bumblebees, who take my messages for me, to come here this evening and fetch the letters. I went out to buy some notepaper, and when I came back my house was gone!'

'Oh dear, I expect someone came along and picked it,' said Bunty, feeling very sorry for the little elf. 'What are you going to do now? You've nowhere to write, have you?'

'No, and all my furniture is gone too,' said the elf sorrowfully. 'If only I could grow another toadstool at once it would be all right, but I can't. It takes a whole night to grow one.'

Bunty thought for a moment, then she had a wonderful idea.

'Do you know, I think I could build you a lovely little house,' she said. 'I could bring my box of dominoes out here and build a house with them. Then I could give you a little chair and table out of my doll's house, and you could sit down and write all your letters beautifully!'

'Oh, you are good!' cried the elf in delight. 'Do you think you could build the house now?'

Bunty ran off to her bedroom. She took her box of

dominoes, a little table and chair, and a cup and saucer from her dolls' tea set, and ran back to the elf. She sat down and found a nice flat piece of grass. Then she began to build a little domino house.

It was rather difficult to build it on the grass, but at last she managed it. It had space left for a window and a nice doorway.

'Could you carry the table and chair in yourself?' Bunty asked the elf. 'I'm afraid I might knock the house down if I try to put them in myself.'

The elf carried them in, and popped the little cup and saucer on the table. He was simply delighted with his new house.

'This is lovely!' he said, sitting himself down at the table. 'Now, I've got my fountain pen, and here's the paper and envelopes I bought this morning. It won't take me long to write out the invitations. I shall be able to have them all ready when the bumblebees call for them this evening.'

Bunty sat down to watch him at work. He wrote

very neatly indeed, and it was lovely to see him sitting at her little doll's house table, in the domino house she had built. All the morning she watched him, then went in for her lunch. She poured lemonade into a thimble and carried it out to the elf. He poured it into his cup and drank it.

'That was good!' he said. 'I was dreadfully thirsty. Thank you so much.'

All the afternoon and after tea Bunty sat and watched the little elf at work. Then suddenly she heard a loud droning noise, and saw a big crowd of furry bumblebees flying down. It really was exciting to see them creep into the domino house and go up to the elf's table. He gave them each a letter.

'Take this to Silvertoes,' he said to one bee. 'Take this to Goldenwings,' he said to another. Bunty could have listened all the evening long – but oh, what a pity, her mother called her to come indoors for supper, and off she had to go.

In the morning she ran to the little house – but it

wasn't there. The elf had neatly taken it to pieces and stacked all the dominoes inside the box. He had put the table and chair on top of the box, beside the cup and saucer, and covered them all with a dock leaf in case it rained.

'Well, I suppose that's the last I shall hear of him!' sighed Bunty, as she picked up the things. 'What fun it was!'

But it wasn't the last she heard – for what do you think! A big bumblebee suddenly flew down and dropped a letter into her lap. Bunty cried out in surprise and opened it.

It was an invitation to the fairy queen's dance!

'Please come on full-moon night to the old oak tree by the pond,' said the letter. 'There will be dancing and games till cockcrow.'

Of course Bunty is going – and wouldn't you love to go with her? I would!

Sailor Jim's
Telescope

Sailor Jim's Telescope

SAILOR JIM had a telescope. He put it on a stand down by the sea wall, and anyone could have a look through it for tenpence.

'We can see the lighthouse as if it was as near as the sea wall!' said Peter.

'And you can see that bird far out to sea just as if it was flying by your nose!' said Lucy.

'And if I look at that far-off boat, I can even see who's in it!' said James. 'It's my cousin Harry and his friend Don!'

Sailor Jim liked the children. He gave them a free peep through his telescope every Saturday morning if they could come and tell him that they had had good marks at school.

And one day George came to tell him a very good piece of news indeed. 'Sailor Jim, what do you think!' he said. 'I've won a scholarship!'

'You don't mean it!' said Sailor Jim. 'Well, well, what brains you must have! Now you tell me what you'd like from me for a reward, and you can have it! A sail in my boat? A fishing trip with me? What would you like to have?'

'Sailor Jim, I suppose you wouldn't lend me your telescope for just one day, would you?' asked George. 'My little sister's ill in bed, and she would so love to have your telescope to look through for a while. She isn't allowed to read. She could look at the birds in the trees, and the sheep far away on the hill – she'd love that!'

'But I wanted to give *you* a reward, not your sister,' said Sailor Jim. 'Surely you would like to go on a fishing trip with me, George?'

'Oh, *yes* – better than anything,' said George. 'But I know how Pat would like your telescope for just one day. She's often said so.'

Sailor Jim didn't know what to say. He really didn't want to part with his telescope for a whole day, especially as there were many people visiting his town now – he would lose a lot of money. But still, he had said that George could ask for what he wanted.

'Right,' he said at last. 'You can take it tomorrow. But be careful of it, won't you?'

George was delighted. How pleased Pat would be! She would feel better at once.

He called for it the next morning and proudly took it off to his sister. She squealed with delight when she saw it and held out her hands. Soon it was propped up on her bed, and she was looking through it.

'The sheep look so big!' she said. 'And now I can see the two little foals properly in the next field. And I can see the rooks pecking up grubs and the shepherd's dog scratching himself. It's like magic! Everything is so near!'

After tea her mother left her by herself with the telescope. George was out in the garden reading. Pat settled down to look through the telescope. She turned it on Mr Land's farm and watched the hens and the ducks there. She turned it on the big field and saw the cows walking through the gate to be milked.

'And now I'll look at that dear little thatched cottage,' she said to herself. The cottage was near a privately owned railway line, and steam trains often went by. Pat could watch the trains with the telescope as well as have a look at the cottage, with its thatched roof and tall hollyhocks.

It's rather like a fairy tale cottage, she thought. *I wonder where the old lady is who lives there? Perhaps she is still having her tea indoors. Oh, here comes a train!*

She heard the rumble and then saw the smoke from the steam engine. The train chugged by the cottage, spitting out smoke and a trail of sparks from its funnel.

It soon disappeared. Pat looked at the cottage through the telescope again. She saw something on the thatched roof. What could it be?

It moved about. Was it a white bird? No, it couldn't be. It grew bigger. It was – yes, it must be – smoke!

'*Smoke!*' said Pat in alarm. 'Smoke on the old cottage's thatched roof! A spark from the engine must have blown there – and it's set light to the dry thatch – the straw has caught alight. Oh dear – the cottage will be burnt down!' The little girl raised her voice and shouted, 'Mummy! MUMMY! Quick, come here!'

Her mother and George came running up at once. 'Look,' cried Pat, pointing out of the window. 'A spark has set the roof of that cottage on fire. It's burning. Call the fire engine, quick! I saw it through the telescope George brought me.'

Mummy flew downstairs to the telephone.

She got on to the fire station at once and told them the news.

'Thanks, madam. The old thatched cottage near the railway, you say? We'll be there in three minutes!'

And so they were! Pat watched the whole thing through the telescope in the greatest excitement. The fire engine raced up. The firemen leapt down. A hose was unrolled, and water began to spray on the burning thatch. And in the middle of it all an old lady came angrily out of her cottage.

'What are you doing? What is the meaning of this?' she cried. The firemen pointed to the smoking roof where the flames were now almost out.

'Your roof was on fire, missus,' said one. 'Just got the warning in time.'

'Who gave the warning?' said the old lady, astonished.

'A little girl called Pat, who lives up in that house over there,' said the fireman, pointing. 'She told her mother and her mother telephoned through to us – and here we are!'

'Thank you, thank you,' said the old lady. 'I must tell my son, and he will go and thank the little girl.'

Who do you suppose her son was? *Sailor Jim.* Wasn't that strange? He was so glad to know that his mother's cottage had been saved that he walked up to George's house that evening and asked to see Pat.

'I'd like to see the little girl who noticed that my mother's roof was on fire,' he said to Pat's mother. 'I want to thank her.'

So up he went into Pat's bedroom – and the very first thing he saw there was his own telescope! He stared at it in astonishment.

'How did you get this?' he asked, picking it up.

'George brought it home for just one day for me to look through – my brother George,' said Pat. 'And it was when I was looking through it after tea that I saw the roof of that cottage smoking. Wasn't it a good thing I had the telescope?'

'It was,' said Sailor Jim. 'A very good thing indeed.

And what a very, *very* good thing I lent it to George because he won a scholarship!'

'Oh! Are you Sailor Jim?' cried Pat. 'George, George, come quickly, here's Sailor Jim!'

George came in and looked astonished to see Sailor Jim. 'Have you come for the telescope?' he asked.

'George, it was Sailor Jim's mother's cottage I saw burning through *his* telescope!' cried Pat. 'Isn't it strange – just like a house-that-Jack-built story!'

Sailor Jim laughed. 'This is the boy who won a scholarship. This is the man who wanted to give him a reward. This is the telescope he lent him. This is the little girl who used it. That's the cottage she saw burning – and here's the man who came to say thank you for saving his mother's home.'

'Oh, Sailor Jim, I'm glad your telescope saved your mother,' said George. 'What a good thing I asked for it!'

'Yes, and I'm giving you something else now,' said Sailor Jim. 'Another reward! Will you both come out fishing with me as soon as this little lady is better?'

'I'll be better tomorrow. I will! I will!' cried Pat.

'You get better by next Saturday and we'll go,' said Sailor Jim.

So Pat is going to get well by then, and off they will all go together to catch plenty of fish for Saturday's supper.

It's strange how things happen, isn't it? You simply never know!

Jinky the Jumping Frog

Jinky the Jumping Frog

JINKY WAS a little green jumping frog who lived in the toy cupboard with all the other toys. He had a spring inside him that made him able to jump high up in the air, and he often frightened the toys by his enormous jumps. He didn't *mean* to frighten them, but, you see, he couldn't walk or run, so his only way of getting about was to jump.

'I'm sorry if I startle you,' he said to the angry toys. 'Please try and get used to my big hops. I can't do anything else you see.'

The toys thought he was silly. He was a shy little frog, and he didn't say much, so the toys thought he was stupid. They left him out of all their games at night, and he was often very lonely when he sat in a corner of the toy cupboard and watched the toys playing with one of the nursery balls.

Now the prettiest and daintiest of all the toys was Silvertoes, the fairy doll. She was perfectly lovely, and she had a silver crown on her head, a frock of finest gauze that stood out all round her, a pair of shining silver wings and a little silver wand which she always carried in her right hand. Everyone loved her, and the green frog loved her the most of all.

But she wouldn't even look at him! He had once made her jump by hopping suddenly down by her, and she had never forgiven him. So Jinky watched her from a distance and wished and wished she would smile at him just once. But she never did.

One night there was a bright moon outside, and the brownie who lived inside the apple tree just by the nursery window came and called on the toys.

'Let's all go out into the garden and dance in the

moonlight,' he said. 'It's lovely and warm, and we could have a fine time together.'

Out went all the toys through the window! They climbed down the apple tree, and slid to the grass below. Then they began to dance in the moonlight. They all took partners except the green frog, who was left out. He sat patiently on the grass, watching the other toys, and wishing that he could dance too.

There was such a noise of talking and laughing that no one noticed a strange throbbing sound up in the sky. No one, that is, except the green frog. He heard it and he looked up. He saw a bright silver aeroplane, about as big as a rook, circling round and round above the lawn.

Then someone looked down from the aeroplane and Jinky shivered with fright – for who should it be but Sly-One, the gnome who lived in Bracken Country, far away. He was a sly and unpleasant person, and nobody, fairy or toy, liked to have anything to do with him.

'I wonder what he wants to come here for tonight!' said Jinky to himself. 'He's up to some mischief, I'm sure!'

He was! He suddenly swooped down in his aeroplane, landed near the toys, ran up to the fairy doll, snatched her away from the teddy bear who was dancing with her and ran off with her to his aeroplane!

How she screamed! 'Help! Help! Oh, please save me, toys!'

The toys were so astonished that they stood and gaped at the bold gnome. He threw the fairy doll into his aeroplane, jumped in himself, and away he went into the air! Then the toys suddenly saw what was happening, and began to shout.

'You wicked gnome! Bring her back at once! We'll put you in prison if you don't!'

The gnome felt quite safe in the air. He circled round and round the toys and bent over the side of his aeroplane to laugh at them.

'Ha, ha!' he said. 'Put me in prison did you say?

Well, come and catch me!'

To the great anger of the toys he flew very low indeed, just above their heads. The teddy bear, who was tall, tried to jump up and hang on to the aeroplane, but he couldn't quite reach it. He was in despair.

'Whatever shall we do?' he cried to the toys. 'We can't possibly rescue the fairy doll in that horrid aeroplane.'

'Ha, ha!' laughed the gnome again, swooping down to the toys – and just at that moment the green frog saw his chance! He would do a most *enormous* jump and see if he could leap right on to the aeroplane.

He jumped. My goodness me, what a leap that was! You should have seen him! He jumped right up into the air, and reached out his front feet for the aeroplane. And he just managed it! He hung on to the tail of the plane, and then managed to scramble up. The gnome had not seen him.

The toys were too astonished to say a word. They

stood with open mouths looking up at the brave green frog, and he signed to them to say nothing about him. He thought that if the gnome did not know he was there, he might be able to rescue the fairy doll without much difficulty.

The gnome flew off in his aeroplane. He wanted to reach Bracken Cottage that night, and he meant to marry the fairy doll in the morning. He thought it would be lovely to have such a pretty creature cooking his dinner and mending his clothes.

The frog crouched down on the tail of the aeroplane. It was very cold there, but he didn't mind. He was simply delighted to think that he would have a chance to do something for the pretty fairy doll.

At last Sly-One arrived at Bracken Cottage. He glided down and landed in the big field at the back of his house. Out he jumped, and turned to the fairy doll, who was cold, frightened and miserable.

'Wait here a minute and I'll just go and unlock the door,' he said. 'Then I'll come back and fetch you.'

He ran off – and as soon as he had gone, the green frog hopped down into the seat beside the fairy doll.

She nearly screamed with fright, but he stopped her.

'Sh!' he said. 'It's only me, Jinky the jumping frog. I've come to save you. Do you think we can fly back in this aeroplane?'

'Oh, Jinky, I'm so glad to see you,' sobbed the poor doll. 'Look, you jerk that handle up, and the aeroplane should fly up into the air.'

Jinky jerked the handle in front of him, but nothing happened. The gnome had stopped the engine, and of course, it wouldn't move. Jinky was in despair. He didn't in the least know how to fly the plane, and he was terribly afraid that if it did begin to fly there would be an accident.

'It's no good,' he said, hopping out of the seat. 'I can't make it go. Come on, fairy doll, get out, and jump on my back. I'll leap off with you, and perhaps we can escape that way.'

'Take the handle out of the aeroplane,' said the doll. 'Then that nasty gnome can't fly after us in it. He won't be able to make it go up!'

'Good idea!' said the frog, and he tore off the handle. He put it into his mouth for he was afraid to throw it anywhere in case the gnome found it again. He thought he would carry it a little way and then throw it into a bush. The fairy doll climbed on to his back, and held tight.

'Now, please, don't be frightened,' said the jumping frog. 'I shall jump high, but you will be quite safe. I can't walk or run, you know.'

'*I* shan't be frightened,' said the fairy doll, clinging to his back. 'I think you are the dearest, bravest, handsomest, strongest frog that ever I saw!'

Well! How Jinky swelled with pride when he heard that! He looked behind him to see that the gnome was still far away – but, oh my goodness, he was running back from his cottage at top speed, for he had seen the doll get out of the aeroplane!

Jinky wasted no more time but leapt high into the air and down again. Again and again he jumped, and each jump took him further away from the gnome, who had gone to his aeroplane to fly after them.

When he found that the starting handle had gone, he was very angry. He jumped out of the plane and ran to his garage. He opened the doors, and in a few moments Jinky heard the sound of a car engine roaring.

Oh, my! he thought in dismay. *If he comes after me in a car, I shan't have any chance at all!*

On he went, leaping as far as he could each time. The fairy doll clung to him, and called to him to go faster still. Behind them came the gnome's car, driven at a fearful speed.

Then crash! There came a tremendous noise and Jinky turned round to see what had happened. The gnome had driven so fast round a corner that he had gone smash into a tree, and his car was broken to pieces. Sly-One jumped out unhurt, very angry indeed. He shook his fist at the jumping frog, and looked at his broken car. Then he ran to a cottage nearby and thumped at the door.

A sleepy goblin came, and asked him what he wanted.

'Lend me your bicycle now!' demanded the gnome. 'I want it to chase a wicked frog.'

The goblin brought it out and the gnome jumped into the saddle. Off he pedalled at a furious rate after the frog and the doll.

'He's got a bicycle now!' shouted the fairy doll to Jinky. 'Oh, hurry up, hurry up!'

Jinky jumped as fast as he could, but the doll was heavy and he began to be afraid that he would never escape. Behind him came the gnome on the bicycle, ringing his bell loudly all the time.

Suddenly the frog came to a village, and in the middle of the street stood a policeman with red wings. He held out his hand to stop Jinky and the doll, but with a tremendous jump the frog leapt right over him and was at the other end of the village before the angry policeman knew what had happened. Then he heard the loud ringing of Sly-One's bicycle bell, and turned to stop the gnome. He held out his hand sternly.

But the gnome couldn't and wouldn't stop! He ran right into the astonished policeman, and knocked him flat on his face. Bump! The gnome flew off his bicycle and landed right in the middle of the duck pond near by. The bicycle ran off by itself and smashed against a wall.

How angry the policeman was! He jumped to his feet and marched over to the gnome. 'I arrest you for not stopping when I told you to, and for knocking me down,' he said.

But the gnome slipped away from him, and ran down the street after the doll and the frog. The policeman ran after him, and off went the two, helter-skelter down the road.

The frog had quite a good start by now, and he was

leaping for all he was worth. The doll was telling him all that had happened, and when he heard how the gnome had run into the policeman, he laughed so much that he got a stitch in his side and had to stop to rest.

'Oh, don't laugh!' begged the doll. 'It really isn't funny. Do get on, Jinky.'

His stitch was soon better, and on he went again, while some way behind him panted the gnome and the policeman. The frog felt sure he could jump faster than the gnome could run, so he wasn't so worried as he had been. For two more hours he jumped and jumped, and at last he came to the place where the toys had been dancing last night. They had all gone back to the nursery, very sad because they felt sure that the fairy doll and the frog were lost for ever.

The frog jumped in at the window, and the fairy doll slid off his back. How the toys shouted and clapped their hands in glee! How they praised the brave frog, and begged his pardon for the unkind things they had said and done to him. And you should have seen his face when the fairy doll suddenly threw her arms around his neck and kissed him! He was so pleased that he jumped all round the room for joy.

Suddenly there was a shout outside. It was the gnome still running, and the policeman after him! The gnome was so angry that he meant to run into the nursery and fight the jumping frog!

Then the teddy bear did a clever thing. He put an empty box just underneath the window, and waited by it with the lid in his hands. The gnome jumped through the window straight into the box, and the bear clapped the lid down on him!

When the policeman came into the room too, the bear bowed gravely to him and handed him the box neatly tied round with string.

'Here is your prisoner,' he said. 'Please take him away, he is making such a noise.'

The surprised policeman thanked the bear, bowed

to the toys, and went out of the window again. Then the toys sat down and had a good laugh, but the one who laughed the loudest of all was Jinky, the little green frog!

The Three
Chocolate Bears

The Three Chocolate Bears

ONCE UPON a time Auntie Sarah bought Jimmy, Jane and Joseph three chocolate bears. They were fine bears, with long noses and big fat legs, made of the loveliest milk chocolate you can imagine.

But Mother wouldn't let the children eat the bears, because she said it would spoil their lunches.

'Well, where shall we put them then?' said Auntie Sarah. 'It's such a terribly hot day that they are sure to melt.'

'Put them in the fridge,' said Mother. 'They will keep nice and hard there.'

So the three bears were put into the fridge. Ooh,

it was cold! It was freezing cold there! The bears began to shiver and shake.

'I say! This is a horrible place to put us!' said the bears. 'They must think we are polar bears! We shall be lumps of ice soon.'

'I'm going to jump out of here as soon as anyone opens the door,' said the biggest bear. 'I can't stand it.'

He didn't have to wait very long. Mother came to get out the butter, and as soon as she opened the fridge, out jumped all the three chocolate bears and ran down the kitchen as fast as they could.

'Ooh my goodness, what's that?' cried Mother in a fright. 'Mice, it must be mice! Now how in the world did they get in there?'

The three bears chuckled to hear themselves called mice. They ran to the boiler and sat down by it.

But Spot, the dog, was lying asleep nearby, and he smelt them in his dream. He woke up, and sniffed. When he saw the chocolate bears he ran to them to eat them. In a terrible fright they rushed out of the kitchen door into the garden. They crept under the back gate, and ran down the path. Spot couldn't follow them because he was too big to get under the gate, and he couldn't open it by himself.

'I still feel very cold,' said the middle bear, shivering. 'If only we could have stayed by that warm boiler!'

'Look! There's a big lump of feathers lying in that ditch!' said the smallest bear. 'Feathers are warm. Let's go and cuddle into them.'

So they ran over to the big lump of feathers and burrowed right into them. Ooh, they were warm! The bears stopped shivering and began to feel happier.

But, oh my goodness, the lump of feathers was a sleeping hen! When she felt the chocolate bears burrowing into her feathers she woke up and looked quite startled. Then she suddenly stood up.

Out dropped the bears with a thud, and the hen clucked in fright. She pecked the ear of the biggest bear and then ran away, squawking loudly.

The three bears were so frightened that they began to shiver again.

'That was a narrow escape,' they said. 'Come on, let's find somewhere else.'

On they went, and soon came to what looked like a big pink wall. They touched it. It was very warm.

'Let's lean up against this,' said the middle bear. 'It's nice and hot.'

So they did – but they hadn't been there very long before the wall shook and shivered and a piggy voice said, 'My gracious, something's tickling me dreadfully!'

And it was a pig! Yes, a fat pink pig lying down in his sty. How scared the three bears were!

'This is dreadful!' they said, scurrying away. 'We were nearly eaten then.'

They rushed out of the sty, and came into a little lane. The sun shone down there and the lane was hot.

'Let's sit down here,' said the biggest bear sleepily. 'That must be a great big fire burning up in the sky.

It will warm us nicely. The grass is so soft here too.'

So they sat down and went to sleep in the sun, and – oh dear, dear me – the sun was so terribly hot that they began to melt. And when they woke up they had melted all away into three little brown chocolate puddles in the grass!

'I can't get up,' said the first bear.

'I haven't any legs,' said the second bear.

'I'm a p-p-p-puddle!' whispered the third bear.

And then a grey donkey came by and licked them all up. 'Funny sort of puddles those were!' said he. 'I wish I could find more like them!'

But he couldn't!

Mary Brown and
Mary Contrary

Mary Brown and Mary Contrary

MARY WAS out for a walk. She took with her Josephine, her biggest doll, and wheeled her in her pram. It was a lovely day, and the sun shone brightly.

Mary went a long way. She walked down the little green path in Bluebell Wood to get out of the hot sun – but dear me, when she turned back she found that she had lost her way!

Somehow or other she must have taken the wrong path – and now she didn't know how to get back. She was most upset.

'Never mind,' she said to herself. 'I shall soon meet someone, and then I can ask them the way to my home.'

In a few minutes she did meet someone. It was a little fat man in a red tunic. He was hurrying along with a hen under his arm. Mary called to him.

'Please,' she said, 'I've lost my way. Can you tell me how to get home?'

'What is your name?' asked the fat man.

'I'm Mary,' said the little girl, 'and this is Josephine, one of my dolls.'

'How do you do, Mary, how do you do, Josephine,' said the little man, raising his pointed cap politely. 'Yes, certainly I can show you your way home. Come with me.'

Mary followed him through the wood, pushing Josephine before her in her pram. She walked down the narrow green path – and at last, to her great surprise, she came out into a little village.

What a strange village! The cottages were very tiny indeed, and at the doors and in the gardens stood children dressed in strange suits and frocks. They looked just as if they had come out of her nursery rhyme book.

Why, those two might be Jack and Jill! thought Mary, looking at a boy and girl who stood holding a pail between them. *And that boy singing all by himself there is just like Tommy Tucker. Look at that girl sitting on a stool too – she's just like Miss Muffet eating her curds and whey!*

'We're nearly there,' said the little man.

'I don't seem to know this way home,' Mary said.

'Don't you?' asked the fat man in surprise, and his hen clucked loudly under his arm, as if she too was surprised. 'Well, here you are. There's your cottage, look!'

Mary looked. They had stopped just outside a trim small cottage whose walls were painted white. At the windows hung bright curtains, and the door was painted yellow. It was a dear little cottage.

'But that isn't my home!' said Mary. 'You've made a mistake!'

'Well, didn't you say that you were Mary?' the little man asked her in astonishment. 'This is Mary's cottage. Look, there's the name on the gate.'

Mary looked. Sure enough, on the gate the words 'Mary's Cottage' were painted.

'And look – there are your cockleshells making a nice border to your flowerbeds,' said the little man, pointing. 'And there are your pretty Canterbury bells, all flowering nicely in the sunshine.'

Mary stared at the cottage garden. She saw that each flowerbed was neatly edged with cockleshells, and that wonderful Canterbury bells flowered everywhere, their blossoms just like silver bells, instead of being blue or white.

'And there are your pretty maids all in a row!' said the little man, waving his hand to where a row of pretty dolls sat on the grass. 'Look, your doll wants to join them.'

To Mary's great astonishment she saw her doll Josephine getting out of the pram! Josephine walked through the garden gate and sat herself down in the row of dolls, who seemed very pleased to see her. Then the wind blew and all the Canterbury bells began to ring – tinkle-tinkle-tinkle!

Mary was too surprised to speak. She couldn't understand it at all – and yet she felt she had seen all this before somewhere. Was it in a book?

'Isn't this your home?' asked the little man, looking puzzled. 'Your name is Mary Quite Contrary, isn't it?'

'No, it isn't!' cried Mary, seeing how he had made his mistake. 'I'm just Mary Brown! You thought I was some other Mary – the Mary of the nursery rhyme. You know: "Mary, Mary, quite contrary, how does your garden grow? With silver bells and cockleshells, and pretty maids all in a row."'

'Well, of course I thought you were!' said the little man. 'I'm so sorry. I've brought you ever so far out of your way.'

Just then the door of the cottage opened and a girl about Mary's age came out. She was a pretty little girl with long curly hair, and she had a big sunbonnet on her head. Her dress reached right to her shoes, and her little feet twinkled in and out as she walked.

'I say, Mary Quite Contrary!' called the little man. 'I've made a dreadful mistake. This little girl's name is Mary, and I've brought her to your cottage thinking she lived here – and she doesn't!'

'Dear me!' said Mary Contrary in a soft little voice. 'What a pity! But never mind – she had better come in and rest for a while and then she shall have lunch with me. I'll see that she gets home all right.'

Mary was delighted. She liked Mary Contrary very much indeed. It would be lovely to have lunch with her. She said goodbye to the little man who had made the mistake, and he hurried off down the street with the hen under his arm clucking loudly.

Mary walked into the garden, and the other Mary took her into her spick-and-span cottage. It was so pretty inside, very small, like a doll's house, but quite big enough for the two children.

'It's so hot that I thought of having ice cream pudding and ginger beer for lunch today,' said Mary

Contrary. 'I hope that will suit you all right, Mary.'

'Oh yes!' said Mary, delighted. 'I think that's just about the nicest lunch I ever heard of!'

Mary Contrary bustled about getting the table laid and Mary Brown helped her. Then they sat down to the largest ice cream pudding Mary had ever seen – and do you know, they finished it between them! Then they had a bottle of ginger beer each. It was really lovely.

'This is the village of Nursery Rhyme,' said Mary Contrary. 'Tom the Piper's Son lives over there – he's a very naughty boy, always in trouble for stealing pigs. I don't have much to do with him! Next door lives Jack Horner, but he has a very good opinion of himself – he's always saying that he is a good boy!'

'Yes, I know all about him,' said Mary Brown. 'Does Humpty Dumpty live here too?'

'Yes,' said Mary Contrary. 'But, you know, he's very silly. He's been warned heaps of times not to sit on walls – but he always will. Then he falls off, and as he is a great big egg he breaks, and there's such a mess to clean up. All the king's horses and all the king's men can't mend him. But he's all right again by the morning – and off he goes to sit on the wall once more!'

'I wish I could see him,' said Mary, excited. 'This is a lovely place, I think. Does Polly Flinders live here too?'

'Yes, but she's a dirty little girl,' said Mary Contrary, wrinkling up her nose in disgust. 'She sits among the cinders and spoils all her nice new clothes. So her mother gets so cross. There is the Black Sheep here too. He doesn't belong to Bo-Peep though – all her sheep are white. She's a silly girl, she's always losing them.'

'But they come home all right, don't they?' asked Mary anxiously.

'Oh yes, and they always bring their tails behind them,' answered Mary Contrary. 'Will you have some more ginger beer? No? Well, now what about getting you home? I'll walk part of the way with you, and perhaps you wouldn't mind giving one of my pretty maids – my dolls, you know – a ride in Josephine's pram for a treat?'

'Of course!' said Mary, smiling. She went to the pram and made room beside Josephine. 'I know Josephine would love to have someone in the pram with her.'

So Mary Contrary tucked Esmeralda, her best pretty maid, into the pram beside Josephine, and the two dolls were very happy to be with one another. Mary loved to see her own doll smiling so cheerfully.

Off the two little girls went. Mary looked excitedly at all the houses she passed. A girl with a red cloak and hood stood at the door of one and Mary felt sure she was Red Riding Hood. She saw Johnny Thin who put the cat in the well, and Johnny Stout, who pulled him out. She waved to the Old Woman who lived in a shoe, and wished she could go nearer to the funny old house in the shape of a shoe and look at it. But she was afraid that the Old Woman might think she was one of her many children, and whip her and put her to bed.

At last they left the strange little village behind and went into the wood. It wasn't very long before they were on the right path to Mary's home.

'Well, you know the way now,' said Mary Contrary, kissing Mary Brown. 'Do come and see me again, won't you? And be sure to bring Josephine with you to visit my pretty maids.'

She took Esmeralda out of the pram, kissed Josephine goodbye and stood waving to Mary as she went along the green path. Mary hurried along, anxious to tell her mother all her adventures.

Mary's mother was surprised! She couldn't believe her ears!

'Well, you come with me, Mummy, next time I go to see Mary Contrary,' promised Mary Brown. 'I know you'll love to see everybody!'

So her mother is going with her tomorrow. I do hope they find the right path, don't you?

Adventure in the Afternoon

Adventure in the Afternoon

IAN HAD a camera. He had had it for his birthday, and he was very pleased with it indeed. It wasn't a new one – it was a very old one, really, that his father had seen in a shop and had bought second-hand.

'New cameras are much too expensive,' he told Ian. 'And, anyway, it is best to learn on an old one – and this is quite a good one. Here's a little instruction book to go with it – it tells you exactly what to do when you want to take a picture.'

Ian was thrilled! A camera! Aha, now he could take his own pictures – and what beauties he would get.

'What are you going to photograph?' said Lisa,

his sister. 'Will you take me, Ian? I'd like you to take a snap of me.'

'Oh, *no*,' said Ian. 'I'm not going to waste my precious films on snapshots of *people*, Lisa. Anybody can do that.'

'Well, what are you going to photograph?' said Lisa. 'Birds? Animals?'

'No,' said Ian. 'They won't keep still enough for me. I'm going to take pictures of cars and trains and aeroplanes. I'm going to make my own book of cars, to begin with. I shall photograph every kind of car! It will be great fun watching out for them and photographing them.'

'Yes. That should be good fun,' said Lisa. 'Are you going to take a picture of our car, Ian? If you do, I could sit at the wheel as if I'm driving it. Do let me.'

So Ian took his first picture – and it was of his father's own car, a Morris, with Lisa sitting up at the wheel as if she were driving it!

He wandered off, with his camera on a strap round his neck. He felt grand with a camera of his own.

But he didn't mean to take the things people usually took. No, he was going to take pictures of the things he was most interested in, and those were cars, planes and trains. Ships too, when he was by the sea.

For the next week Ian had a fine time. He took a picture of a beautiful Rolls Royce, complete with a very grand chauffeur. He took a picture of a tiny little baby car with a dog at the back. It had been left there to guard the car, and it barked loudly and fiercely at Ian when he came up with his camera.

'Don't you want your picture taken?' said Ian, and he clicked the camera. 'Well, I've taken it! And if you come out on it with your mouth wide open, barking madly, don't blame *me*.'

When he had finished the whole film his father showed him how to develop each picture. Soon Ian had twelve beautiful pictures of cars to stick into his car book. He was very proud and pleased.

'You've really done well with your first film,' said his father in surprise.

'Well, I read that little book of instructions carefully first,' said Ian, 'and did exactly what it said.'

'Sensible of you,' said his father. 'Most people rush at a new thing – they don't trouble to learn anything about it first, and then they wonder why they get poor results. You deserve your camera, Ian.'

Ian went on with his photographing of all kinds of cars. He got Austins and Bentleys, and Rileys and Standards and Rovers and Vauxhalls – in fact, all the cars you see rushing about on the roads each day. I expect you know as many as he did.

He stuck the pictures of them in his book. 'I've got nearly every make of car now,' he told his father. 'I've got American cars too – and look, that's a French one – and there's another. I haven't got an Italian one yet. There's room for that, if only I can get one. They're lovely cars, aren't they, the Italian ones?'

His father didn't know as much about cars as Ian did, and he laughed. 'Funny hobby, this, of yours,' he said to Ian. 'I don't know that it's much use, really;

it's fun for you, of course, but, honestly, your book looks rather like a catalogue of second-hand cars.'

Ian didn't mind. He enjoyed his hobby, and he loved taking his camera out, ready to snap any new or unusual car that he saw. It was fun to snap them and even more fun to develop the film and see what kind of picture he had got.

One afternoon he was sitting by the roadside, waiting for cars to come by. There was a lovely view to be seen from the place he had chosen and cars often pulled up to look at it. Then Ian could snap them if they were cars he wanted.

It was very hot indeed. Ian moved out of the sun and snuggled into the greenery of the hedge. His eyes shut. He was asleep!

He was awakened by the sound of a car pulling up near to him. He opened his eyes, yawned and poked his head out of the shady greenery around. Then he sat up straight in delight.

An Italian car! A real beauty – a big yellow one

with bright silver lines shining here and there. What a car! Just what he wanted for his book of car photographs.

He pulled his camera case over to him and took out his camera. He saw a man get out of the car and walk to the wall on the other side of the road. He had something in his hand, but Ian couldn't see what it was.

To the boy's surprise the man lifted his hand and threw what he was holding over the wall. Then he walked back to the car. *They'll be off again in half a jiffy*, thought Ian. *I must snap the car at once or I'll miss it. What a beauty! I might never see such a fine Italian car again!*

He hurriedly knelt up on one knee and squinted down at the little camera mirror that told him whether the car was in his picture or not. It was – right in the middle, shining beautifully in the sun. The man was just walking over to it.

Click! Ian snapped down the little lever that took

the picture, and at the same moment the driver revved up his engine – *rrrrrr-rrrrrr-rrrr!*

The car shot off at top speed. Nobody had spotted Ian in the shade of the hedge. Nobody had heard the click of his camera. How Ian hoped that his picture would come out well! What a beautiful car to add to the collection in his car book!

He was walking home, longing to develop his roll of film and see what the picture of the Italian car was like, when he saw a white car coming along in the distance. Ian saw a sign glowing on it: POLICE.

'A police car,' he said to himself, 'and jolly fast too, I should think. I wish they'd stop, because I've got just one more picture to take on this film – and although I've got plenty of Wolseleys, I've never had one yet with POLICE showing on it.'

Just as if the car had heard his wish, it slowed down and stopped beside him! Ian hurriedly took his camera out of his case. Now, he could snap this police car.

But before he could snap the car, a uniformed policeman put his head out of the window. 'Hey, sonny! Seen any cars along here lately?'

'Only one in the last half hour,' said Ian. 'I fell asleep in the hedge.'

The policeman gave an exclamation of annoyance. 'Well, you won't be much help then. What was the car you saw?'

'An Italian car,' said Ian. 'It stopped just by me, and the noise of the engine woke me up.'

'Ha! Good!' said the policeman. 'Then you can tell me who was in the car – how many, and what they were like.'

'Oh, no, I can't tell you that,' said Ian, trying to think hard. 'I didn't notice. I just saw a man get out of the car and throw something over the wall down there – some rubbish, I suppose – and then he got back and the car drove away at once.'

'What was the man like?' asked the policeman.

'I don't know,' said Ian. 'I really didn't notice, sir.'

'Think of that!' said the policeman in an exasperated voice, turning to another man in the car. 'Here's a boy who had a good chance of seeing how many there were in the car, what they were like and everything – and all he knows is what the car looked like!'

Ian felt hurt at the man's tone. 'Well, sir, I know you think I'm jolly stupid,' he said. 'But actually I was photographing the car for my car book – so naturally I didn't bother about the people in it.'

Then things happened very quickly!

The three policemen in the car exclaimed loudly, one of them hauled Ian into the car and another whipped his camera case off his shoulder!

'He may have got just what we want!' said one of them. 'We'll get the snap developed immediately! Johns, you drop off at the wall where this youngster says he saw one of the men throw something over, and see what you can find. We'll drive on to the police station and get this film developed at once.'

'But it's *my* film!' began Ian indignantly. 'I always

develop my own films. What's all the excitement about?'

'Well, you deserve to know, seeing that it is likely you may be going to present us with a photograph of one or two people who are concerned in a robbery of valuable state papers,' said the first policeman. 'We've an idea who they are, but we've no proof at the moment. All we know is that they drove off in a big Italian car.'

Now it was Ian's turn to get excited! Fancy his camera snapping the very car with the robbers in – and maybe the very robbers themselves. Ian remembered the man who had been walking towards the car just when he had snapped it. Surely he would be in the picture?

One of the policemen dropped off at the wall and jumped over it to see what he could find. He hoped to get the case in which the stolen papers had been kept. It would be empty, of course – but there might be fingerprints on it.

The police car sped on to the big police station in

the next town. The film was taken from Ian's camera and was soon being developed in a little darkroom. Ian watched in excitement.

At last one of the policemen gave a whistle and held up the roll of film to the light. 'Look here! This is the car – and who's that beside it? It's Lennie Richardson, isn't it? We thought he was in on this. And look, here's a man at the wheel, he's come out plainly – my word, it's Pete Lucien!'

'Is it a good snap?' asked Ian, patiently trying to get a peep of it.

'Fine! Couldn't be better!' said the policeman. 'What a bit of luck for us! Got the car *and* the men all in one picture – absolutely positive proof of the thieves concerned. Sonny, you did much better than you know when you snapped that car!'

Well, what a thrill for Ian! The thieves were caught because of his picture, and in the newspapers the next day was the photograph he had taken of the car and the men!

Ian was so proud that he couldn't stop talking about it.

'Fancy my little old camera taking a picture so valuable as that!' he kept saying. 'What a fine picture I've got to put in my car book – the best and most exciting of the lot.'

All the newspapers that printed Ian's car picture paid him a fee for it – and to his enormous surprise the boy soon had more money than he had ever had in his life!

'Almost ten pounds!' he said. 'Well, I know what I'm going to do with it!'

I know too, don't you? He's going to buy a really magnificent camera now, for a train book. If ever you meet him, ask him to show you his car book – it's really very interesting indeed. *Especially* the last two pictures in the book – a big Italian car, shining in the sun, and a gleaming white car with a word showing clearly: POLICE.

Tommy's White Duck

Tommy's White Duck

TOMMY HAD a real live duck of his own. He had had it given to him when it was just a little yellow duckling, and somehow or other nobody had ever thought what it would be like when it grew up!

At first it was just a dear little yellow bird, crying, 'Peep, peep, peep!' all day. Tommy's father made it a tiny run of its own, with wire netting all round, and a small coop for it to sleep in. Tommy fed it and gave it a little bowl of water to swim in.

And then, quite suddenly it seemed, it began to grow! By the time the middle of the summer came it was quite a big duck. It had lost its pretty yellow down and grew snowy-white feathers. It no longer said, 'Peep, peep!' but quacked quite loudly.

Father had to make the run bigger. The days went on, and the duck grew and grew. It could no longer swim in the bowl, nor even in the tin bath which Mother put out for it.

'Daddy, could we make a little pond for my duck to swim in?' asked Tommy one day. 'I could help you dig it out, couldn't I?'

'Dear me, I'm not going to dig a pond for the noisy old duck!' said his father. 'It's got too big for us now, Tommy. We shall have to sell it.'

'Daddy!' cried Tommy, his eyes full of tears. 'Sell my duck! Oh, I couldn't! Why, perhaps somebody would have it for their dinner – it would be simply dreadful!'

'Well, Tommy, it's really too big now,' said his father. 'Besides, it has such a noisy quack.'

'But, Daddy, if we made it a little pond of its own, it would be happy and wouldn't quack so much,' said Tommy. 'I'm sure that's why it's quacking such a lot – because it wants a swim.'

'Well, then, what about letting the farmer's wife have the duck back?' asked Father. 'She gave it to you when it was a duckling, and maybe she'd like it back now, to go with her other ducks. Then it could swim on her big pond.'

Tommy didn't say any more. He could see that his father didn't want the duck, and that it would have to go. But he was very sad about it, and he went to the garden to talk to the duck.

'Quack!' said the duck joyfully when it saw Tommy.

'Hallo,' said Tommy. 'Dear old duck, I'm afraid you're going to be given away, and won't live with me any more.'

'Quack!' said the duck, and gave Tommy a small, loving peck.

Well, the very next day the duck was taken down the lane to the farm, and Tommy had to say goodbye to it. The duck seemed very puzzled, but when it saw the other ducks it went quite mad with joy and dashed into the pond, waddling so fast that it fell over its own big flat feet!

'There you are!' said Father, turning to Tommy. 'See how pleased the duck is to be here!'

'But it will miss me when it's got used to being here,' said Tommy. 'It will want me, Daddy.'

'Nonsense!' said his father, laughing, and he took Tommy home.

Well, it so happened that Tommy was right, for the very next day the duck had a look round and thought, *Where's Tommy? Where's my own run? Where's the garden I know so well? Where, oh where, is Tommy?*

The duck sat in the sun and thought. It loved Tommy and wanted to be with him. So what did it do but walk over the farmyard and squeeze under the gate, and set off waddling up the lane, back to Tommy's house and garden!

'Quack!' it said as it went. 'Quack!' Up the dusty

lane it went, and at last it came to Tommy's house. Nobody was in. Tommy was at school. Tommy's father was at work. Tommy's mother had slipped in the house next door to talk to Mrs White. But the baby was in her pram in the garden fast asleep.

'Quack!' said the duck, squeezing through the hedge and looking round for Tommy. But just then something happened. There came the sound of thundering hooves and two of the farm horses galloped up the lane!

Someone had left the field gate open, and the horses had got out. They were excited and were running after one another. And what do you think happened? Why, one of them saw the garden gate open and galloped through into the garden!

The duck knew quite well this was wrong. Suppose the horse knocked the pram over? Good gracious, look at the mess it was making of the lovely lawn, sinking its hard hooves deep into the grass!

There was only one thing to do, and the duck knew

what it was! It knew quite well that usually when it quacked loudly, Tommy's mother came to the window and said, 'Sh! Sh! You'll wake the baby!' And if only the duck could make her come, she would see the galloping horse and everything would be put right! The duck didn't know that Tommy's mother was not in the house, of course.

It began to quack. How it quacked! You should have heard it! 'Quack, quack, quack, quack, QUACK, QUACK, QUACK!'

Tommy's mother heard the loud quacking from the next-door house. 'Well!' she said in surprise. 'That sounds just like our duck – but it can't be, because Tommy and his father took it down to the farm yesterday.'

'Quack, quack, quack, quack, quack, QUACK, QUACK!' cried the duck, as the horse galloped round the garden once more.

'It must be our duck!' said Tommy's mother and she ran back home to see – and, of course, she at once saw the horse in the garden!

'Oh! Oh!' she cried. 'It will knock the pram over! It will knock the pram over!'

She caught up a stick and ran to the excited horse. She drove it to the gate – and it went out at a gallop, off down the lane to the farm, where the other horse had also gone.

Mother shut the gate. She was quite pale and frightened. Tommy came running home from school and wondered what was the matter.

'Oh, Tommy!' said Mother. 'One of those great farm horses got into the garden this afternoon when I was next door, and nearly knocked the pram over!'

'But how did you know it was here, galloping about?' asked Tommy. 'Did you hear the baby crying?'

'No, I heard your old duck quacking!' said his mother. 'Fancy that, Tommy! It must have walked all the way up the lane to get back to you – and it quacked loudly when it saw the horse, and warned me.'

'Oh, you good old duck!' cried Tommy, running to

his duck and putting his arms round its snowy neck. 'You good old thing! You saved the baby! Oh, Mother, I do wish we could keep my duck! Look how it's come all the way home again!'

'You shall keep it,' said Mother, and she patted the surprised duck on the head. 'When I tell Daddy about how it warned me this afternoon by quacking so loudly, he will be sure to say it can stay with you now.'

So Tommy's mother told his father – and what do you think he and Tommy are doing this week? Guess!

Yes, they are both digging out a nice little pond for the duck, for it is to stay with Tommy, of course. Won't it be pleased to have a pond of its own! Yesterday it laid its first egg – and Father had it for breakfast!

'Quack!' said the duck. 'I'm one of the family. You can't get rid of me! Quack!'

The Girl Who Was Left Behind

The Girl Who Was Left Behind

'TOMORROW WE'RE going for a day by the sea, by the sea!' sang the children in Miss Williams's class.

'Well, mind you are none of you late for the coach,' said Miss Williams, gathering up her books. 'The coach will be at the town hall at ten o'clock. It will wait for ten minutes only, then it will start. So you must all be very punctual!'

'We'll be there before the bus!' said Millie.

'We'll be ten minutes early!' cried John.

'I'll have to do my mother's shopping first, but I can get there by ten o'clock,' said Alice.

They all went home, happy because they were to

have a day's holiday by the sea tomorrow. Paddling, bathing, digging – what fun they would have!

All the children were up early the next day. It was Saturday. Most of them had little jobs to do. They had to make their own beds. They had to tidy up their toys. They had to feed chickens, or perhaps help with the shopping.

'I'm off to do my mother's shopping now,' said Alice, peeping over the fence at Millie, who was sitting reading in her garden. 'Wait for me, won't you? I'll be back as soon as I can. Then we'll run together to the town hall to get into the coach.'

'I'll wait for you,' promised Millie. 'But don't be late, for goodness' sake!'

Alice set off. There was a lot of shopping to do, and the shops were full. She stood for a long time at the greengrocer's, but at last she was served. Then on she went to the baker's and to the chemist's.

She looked at a clock. Half past nine. She must hurry home now, because she had to put on a clean dress. She would just have enough time.

She hurried home. She gave her mother the shopping and counted out the change. She was a good, sensible little girl, and her mother trusted her with a lot of things.

Then she went upstairs to put on a clean dress. But, oh dear, it had a button missing! Never mind, there was just time to sew it on. Alice got out her needle and cotton.

Soon she heard Millie coming in from next door and calling up the stairs.

'Do come, Alice. It's five to ten! Do come. I shan't wait for you.'

'Coming, coming!' cried Alice, and slipped her dress over her head. She buttoned it quickly, picked up her bag and ran downstairs. She kissed her mother goodbye, and ran out with Millie.

'It's ten o'clock already,' said Millie. 'The coach will be there. We shan't get the best seats.'

They ran down the street. Just as they got to the

corner a boy came round on a bicycle. A dog ran across the road, and the front wheel of the bicycle ran into him. The dog yelped. The boy fell off his bicycle with a crash, and the bicycle fell on top of him. He lay still, stunned for a moment.

The girls stopped in alarm. Alice ran to the boy. He opened his eyes and sat up, rubbing his knee, which was bruised and bleeding. 'I feel funny,' he said. 'I've hurt my knee. Oh, look at my poor bicycle. I can't ride it home. The front wheel is bent. And all the things have fallen out of my bag. Could you pick them up for me, please?'

He was a boy about Alice's age, but she did not know him. She began to pick up the spilt things. Millie wouldn't help.

'Alice! We simply can't stop! Let someone else help him! We've got to catch that coach!'

'You help me then, and we'll be able to,' said Alice. 'You pick up the things, and I'll help the boy up. Go on, Millie.'

'What, and miss the coach that is going to take us to the sea!' cried Millie. 'It's five past ten already! I'm going. Are you coming or not, Alice?'

'Oh, yes, yes, just wait a minute. I can't leave this boy till he can stand up properly and wheel his bike,' said Alice anxiously. 'There's nobody else about to help him. You go on, Millie, and just tell Miss Williams I'll be along in a minute. Don't let the coach go without me.'

Millie ran off, looking cross. How silly of Alice to mess about like that! Let the boy help himself! He wasn't badly hurt. He could easily pick up his own things. Well, even if Alice was going to miss the coach, Millie wasn't!

She tore round the corner and ran down to the town hall. Thank goodness, the coach was still there. All the other children were in it. Miss Williams was standing beside it, looking anxiously for Millie and Alice.

'Where's Alice?' she said.

'Oh, she's messing about round the corner!' said Millie unkindly. 'She just won't be quick. I did tell her we'd be late. I left her behind.'

'The naughty little girl,' said Miss Williams, looking at her watch. 'I'll wait one more minute, and then we shall go.'

Alice helped the boy to his feet. He seemed a bit better. All his things were soon back in his bag. His bicycle could not be ridden so he would have to wheel it home.

'You sit down on that wall over there for a few minutes before you wheel your bike home,' said Alice, 'then you'll feel well enough. I'm sorry I can't stay and see you home, very sorry, but you see, the coach will only wait until ten minutes past ten.'

She ran off and the boy looked after her, thinking what a kind little girl she was. It was nice to find someone kind when you were hurt and dizzy. Kindness was one of the best things in the world.

Alice rushed round the corner and looked

anxiously at the town hall, which she could see from there. There was no coach waiting for her! It had gone! Yes, there it was, climbing the hill beyond. It hadn't waited.

Alice stood and looked after it. It hadn't waited. Just because she had stopped to be kind, she had missed a lovely day by the sea. Millie, who hadn't been kind at all, had caught the coach.

'But I couldn't help stopping to help that boy,' said Alice. 'I just couldn't. And now the coach has gone without me.'

Tears came to her eyes and trickled down her cheek. She had hurried so much, she had done all the shopping, she had had plenty of time to get to the coach – and yet she was left behind.

She turned to go home. She had forgotten about the boy sitting on the wall. She did not see him as she walked past him, her tears blinding her. She gave a little sob. She was so dreadfully, dreadfully disappointed.

The boy saw her in surprise. Hadn't she told him she was going to catch a coach? Surely it hadn't gone without her!

'Hi!' he called. 'What's the matter? Come over here and tell me.'

So Alice told him, and then it was the boy's turn to comfort poor Alice. 'What a shame!' he said. 'I stopped you from catching the coach. Oh, I do feel dreadful about it. Poor, poor Alice.'

'I can go home with you now, and wheel your bicycle, if you like,' said Alice, wiping her eyes. 'You look rather pale, and you ought to have your knee bathed. Come along.'

So she took the boy home, wheeling his bicycle for him. He lived in a lovely house about three streets away. His mother was in the garden, and came running to meet him.

'What have you done, Donald? Oh, your poor knee. What has he done, what happened?'

Alice told her. Then Donald told his mother how

Alice had helped him. She was so grateful.

'Come along in and have some lemonade,' she said. 'I'll just bathe Donald's knee. I don't think it's really very bad.'

While his mother was bathing his knee, Donald told her how poor Alice had missed the coach because she had stayed to help him. 'So there will be no day by the sea for her,' he said. 'And all because of me!'

His mother looked thoughtful. Then she smiled. 'Alice shan't miss her day by the sea!' she said. 'I will take her, and you too, in the car! It will do you good to have a blow by the sea, after this nasty little fall. We will go to your Auntie Lou's for the day and have a lovely time! Would you like that?'

'Oh, yes!' said Donald, cheering up at once. 'Shall I go and tell Alice? Have you finished with my knee? Oh, won't she be pleased!'

Alice was. She could hardly believe her ears. After her big disappointment it seemed too good to be true that she was going to have a day by the sea after all!

She thanked Donald's mother shyly, and her eyes shone with joy.

They soon set off in Donald's mother's little car. First they went round to Alice's mother and told her. She was very surprised, but pleased to know that Alice had been so kind.

Then off they went. It was a fast little sports car, and Donald's mother drove well. Alice enjoyed it. She had never been in a sports car before, and she thought it was lovely.

'We're going so fast,' she said. 'Do you think we'll pass the coach that the others are in?'

'Well, they had a good start,' said Donald's mother. 'We may get there about the same time.'

The funny thing was, they did! Just as the car drew up on the seafront for the two children to look at the calm blue sea, a big coach drew up too – and it was the one with all the schoolchildren in!

'Look! There's Alice! Surely that's Alice!' Millie cried in amazement. 'Alice, Alice, how did you get here? We left you behind!'

She jumped down and ran to Alice. But Donald did not welcome her. 'This is the other girl who saw me fall,' he said to his mother. 'But she didn't help. She just stood and said they would miss the coach, and ran off without Alice, and she didn't even get the coach to wait!'

Millie went red. She knew she had been selfish and unkind. She went back to the others, still red. Now she wished she had been kind too! Here was Alice, going to have a lovely day with Donald's nice mother – and going back in a sports car! And Millie had thought her so silly to stay behind and help.

Alice had a wonderful day. Donald's Auntie Lou was as kind as his mother, and they all four had a picnic on the beach and ice creams afterwards. They had ice creams again at teatime, and Donald and Alice had three rides each on a donkey, and a lovely bathe.

'Now we must go home,' said Donald's mother, who had been watching Alice and thinking what a well-mannered, nice little girl she was. 'Come along.'

'Oh, I wish the day wasn't over!' said Alice with a sigh. 'I have so loved it.'

'We'll have more days like this,' said Donald's mother. 'You must come to tea with Donald every week. You will be a nice friend for him – someone who is kind and unselfish. Donald is kind too, so you will make a good pair!'

They do, and they are very happy playing together. 'Your bit of kindness brought you a big reward,' Alice's mother said. It certainly did, but I think Alice deserved it, don't you?

Adventure for Two

Adventure for Two

'COMING WITH me in the car?' called Daddy to Philip and Mary. 'I'm just going down to see old Mrs Blakey.'

'Oh, is she ill?' said Mary. Her daddy was a doctor and went to see ill people every day.

'No, not ill. She's sprained her ankle, that's all,' said Daddy. 'I'm just going to have a look at it – and then I rather thought I'd go to the bakery and have one of those chocolate ice creams of theirs. But you know how I hate eating ice creams alone.'

'Oooh, Daddy! Of course we'll come!' said Philip. He came running out of the playroom with Mary.

'You're a great daddy! You always tell us when you're going ice-creaming!'

They went to get their coats. Their father went out to get his car. He brought it into the front drive.

Philip and Mary came running out. 'I'll go in the front now, and you can be there coming back,' said Mary to Philip. In they got, and off went the car. Down the drive, out into the road and up the hill. Down the hill and round the corner – and there was old Mrs Blakey's house, with its thick yew hedge all round the front garden.

'Now you just look after my car for me while I'm in the house,' said Daddy, 'then I shan't need to lock it up. I always have to if there's nobody in it, because my precious case of medicines might be stolen.'

'Oh, yes,' said Philip. 'And some of them are very poisonous, aren't they?'

Daddy went up the path to the house. The children sat in the car, looking at the thick yew hedge. Mary got out.

'I just want to look at the hedge,' she said to Philip. 'It's so very, very thick. Why, it's thick enough to get right into the middle of it!'

Philip got out too. They had always liked old Mrs Blakey's thick yew hedge. Mary parted the green boughs and looked into the depths of the dark hedge.

'Philip!' she said. 'Look! There's a kind of passage going right along the middle of the hedge!'

Philip looked. It did really seem like a passage! The leaves there had dried and fallen off, and the middle of the hedge was empty and bare.

'We could almost go along it,' said Philip. 'Mary, shall we just get into it for a minute? I believe if we were in the very middle, nobody could possibly see us! What a wonderful hiding place it would make!'

'Let's hide from Daddy!' said Mary at once. 'That *would* be fun! He'd come out and look for us – and we wouldn't be there!'

'And we could say something in a very deep, hollow kind of voice,' said Philip. 'It would make him jump!

Come on, Mary, before he comes out.'

It was easy to squeeze into the thick yew hedge. Once in the centre the branches closed firmly round them, and nobody could see them.

'But I've got a fine peephole, Mary – have you?' asked Philip. 'I can see Daddy's car through it.'

'Yes. I've got a peephole too – between some leaves,' said Mary. 'Philip, supposing somebody comes by – had we better keep still and quiet?'

'Yes,' said Philip. 'We can't give our hiding place away!'

'I can hear someone coming now,' said Mary, and she looked through her peephole. 'It's Jimmy White!'

Jimmy passed by, whistling cheerfully. Philip and Mary giggled. They longed to say, 'Beware, Jimmy!' in a deep, peculiar voice, but they knew Jimmy well enough to know that he would at once go to look in the hedge for the voice!

'Now there's a woman coming,' whispered Philip. 'I don't know her.'

The woman passed, walking quickly. The children sat quite still in their hiding place. The passerby didn't know anyone was so near her!

Nobody came for a little while. Then Philip heard soft footsteps. He peeped out.

'Two men, Mary,' he whispered. 'Aren't they walking quietly!'

The men came up to the car – but they didn't walk past. They stopped just by it. The children held their breath in case their hiding place should be discovered.

'No one about,' said one man in a very low voice. 'Whose car's this? It's got a case inside.'

'It's Dr Fenton's car,' said the other man in such a low voice that the children could hardly hear him. 'That will be his case. There will be valuable drugs in there. Any chance of getting them?'

'Better try now, while there's no one to see,' said the first man. He wrenched the front door of the car open and put his hand in quickly. In a second he had taken the case and had shut the door quietly.

Then the two men moved off quickly, walking very softly.

The children had seen all this, and were absolutely thunderstruck. Two robbers! Thieves who had dared to open their father's car and take his case – in full daylight too! Well, you read of such things in the newspapers – but they never, never happened under your nose like this!

'Mary!' said Philip, finding his tongue at last. 'We didn't do a thing. We never even shouted.'

'I couldn't,' said Mary. 'It all happened so quickly. What are we going to do? Daddy's case is gone.'

'And we were supposed to be in charge of it,' said Philip, horrified at the thought. 'Goodness, we were pretty feeble, Mary. If only we'd just given one shout, those men would have shot off at once, without even opening the car.'

'Yes, but it all happened so *quickly*,' said Mary, almost in tears. 'I couldn't say a word. I did try, but I couldn't. Let's get out of this hedge and tell Daddy.'

At that very moment they heard the front door slam, and their father came briskly down the path.

'Now what about our ice creams?' he called, as he got to the gate.

Philip and Mary were just climbing out of the hedge. They looked untidy and were covered with little bits and pieces. They looked so very solemn that their father was surprised.

'I say, did you *have* to climb into that dirty old hedge?' he said, opening his car. Then he stopped and stared. 'Good gracious – where's my case gone?'

'Daddy, it's been stolen,' said Philip. 'Oh, Daddy, it was our fault. We were in the hedge when the men came by and we . . .'

'Now begin at the beginning and tell me everything,' said Daddy, seeing at once that something serious had happened. So the two children told him everything: how they had got into the hedge, how people had come by, and the two men had come and talked, and then had stolen the case.

'Did they see you?' asked Daddy. 'Did they know you were there?'

'Oh, no,' said Philip. 'But we saw *them* all right. We know exactly what they are like and how they are dressed. If we saw them again we'd know them.'

'Very well then – hop quickly into the car,' said Daddy. 'I'll go to the police station and collect a policeman in plain clothes, and we'll drive slowly around and about the streets. Maybe we'll see those men again!'

This was all very exciting indeed. The children got into the car, and Daddy drove off. He went first to the police station, then quickly told what had happened, and was given an extra passenger – a policeman dressed in ordinary clothes.

'They'll have wrapped up that case of yours in brown paper by now, sir,' said the policeman. 'No good looking for the case – have to look for a large brown-paper parcel, or a suitcase big enough to have put your case in. They wouldn't be foolish enough to carry your bag openly for long. Good thing these youngsters of yours noticed what the men were like!'

The car drove slowly down one street and up another. 'There are two men,' said the policeman suddenly. 'Sitting on that seat, sir; look – with a big parcel.'

'No, that's not the men,' said Philip. 'Is it, Mary? Our men had different clothes – one was in a brown suit with a brown tie, and the other was in a green jacket with a black tie.'

'Right. Go on again, sir, please,' said the policeman. 'Ah, wait – what about these men coming round the corner with a case?'

The men had on the right-coloured suits, but they were not a bit like the ones the children had seen.

'No, both those men are small,' said Mary, 'and our men are tall. One had a little moustache and the other hadn't. And they both wore hats like Daddy's, and one man had a tiny feather stuck into his hatband.'

'My word, these kids of yours notice a lot, don't

they?' said the policeman, most impressed. 'They'll be telling us how many toes the men had next!'

The children laughed. They were keeping a very close lookout indeed. They had felt so ashamed of letting those men steal their father's case under their very noses; now they felt they really must catch them and get the case back, or they would never forgive themselves.

Up the hill and down. No men at all. Round the town and back again. Plenty of men, but not the ones they wanted.

'Of course they might have gone into a shop somewhere, or the cinema,' said the policeman. 'They've had time to get a good way away now, and unless they caught a bus or a train they'll probably be sitting down having tea somewhere – or seeing a film. I'm afraid we'll have to give up finding them this way, sir. I've got all the particulars from the children – though I'd like to ask them a few questions – and we'll send out descriptions of the men everywhere.'

'Right,' said Dr Fenton. 'Well, would you like to come along to my house and ask the children what else you want to know?'

Mary spoke up in a very small voice, 'Daddy, I suppose we don't deserve those ice creams now, do we?'

'Bless us all!' said Daddy. 'I'd quite forgotten we were going to have some. Yes, of course we'll have them. Constable, will you join us? You can ask your questions in the bakery.'

'Yes, sir. It would be quite a treat,' said the policeman, beaming round at the two children. 'It's a long time since I was taken to have an ice cream.'

They came to the bakery, and they got out. This time Daddy locked his car well and truly. 'Though it's rather like locking the stable door after the horse has gone,' he told the children. 'Come along.'

They went into the tearoom of the bakery, but it was teatime now and the place was full. 'I've a little room upstairs,' said the shop woman. 'I think there's a table up there, sir.'

So up they went and found the table. A girl came to take their order. While they were waiting for their ice creams the two children looked round the room. They had never been in this little room before, and they didn't think it was as nice as the big one downstairs. Still, the ice creams would be just as good!

Mary suddenly trod hard on Philip's toe. Philip looked at her in surprise. Then he looked where she was looking, and he went bright red with excitement.

Sitting huddled together in the darkest corner of the little room were the two men who had stolen their father's case! There was no mistaking them at all – one with a moustache, one with none; one with a green jacket and black tie, and the other in brown with a brown tie.

And under the table was a very large suitcase! The children looked at one another. They didn't dare to whisper their news in case the men suspected something. So Philip took out his little notebook and pencil and scribbled something in it. He passed it silently to his father.

'Those are the men over there. Look at the suitcase under the table!' That was what he had written.

His father passed the note to the policeman, who looked casually over at the two men. He in turn scribbled a note very quickly and had it ready for the girl when she came with their ice creams. His note was short and clear.

'Take this to the police station,' was written on the outside. And inside: 'Send two men to Harrison's Bakery at once. Upstairs. Johns.'

The girl brought their ice creams, took the note, looked at the outside, seemed very scared and went out quickly. Two other people finished their tea and went. That left only the two men and the children's table.

The girl came back and slid a note into the policeman's hands. One of the two men called out to her.

'Hey, miss – what times does the bus to Highlands go?'

'Not for fifteen minutes, sir,' said the girl.

Good, thought the children. *The men won't slip out yet.*

Two strange men came into the tearoom and sat down silently at the table next to the children's. They nodded to the policeman, who at once got up and went over to the two men.

'I have reason to think that there is stolen property in that case of yours,' he said. 'Will you open it?'

The men leapt up at once, blustering angrily. One caught up the case. 'What cheek!' he said. 'Who are you to say things like that! I'll report you to the police.'

'I *am* the police,' said the policeman stolidly. 'Open that case, please.'

The men pushed him aside and went to the door. But the other two policemen were there now. No escape that way!

'Huh! Three of you!' said one of the men in disgust. 'All right. Open the case. Though how you know it was us that did the job I don't know. There wasn't anyone to see.'

'Walls have ears,' said the policeman, opening the case and taking out Dr Fenton's bag from inside. 'And hedges have eyes!'

Well, of course, the two men had no idea what he was talking about, but the children knew! They were pleased to see the two men marched off.

'I'm glad you've got your bag back, Daddy,' said Mary. 'We were silly to let it be stolen. What a good thing we came here for ice creams!'

'It was,' said Daddy. 'I say, what about another one each just to celebrate your exciting adventure!'

The Land of
Nowhere

The Land of Nowhere

DANIEL AND Susie had a pet between them. They loved it very much indeed. It was a pure white rabbit with big, floppy ears and a lovely nose that twitched up and down. They called it Snowball, and every day they gave their rabbit fresh lettuce to eat and cleaned out its hutch.

'He's the loveliest rabbit in the world,' Daniel said, and Susie thought so too. The children had no other pets – just Snowball; so they loved the rabbit very much, and played with him as often as they could.

Then one day a dreadful thing happened. They went to Snowball's hutch after breakfast – and the door was wide open. Daniel peeped into the hutch and looked all round. There was no rabbit there!

'Susie!' he cried. 'What's happened? Snowball's gone! However could he have opened the door?'

'He couldn't have,' said Susie in astonishment. 'I shut it myself yesterday evening and made it fast. I remember doing it.'

'Yes, I saw you,' said Daniel. 'Then how could Snowball have escaped?'

'Somebody let him out,' said Susie, nearly crying.

'Oh, it's too bad! Let's look for him.'

So they looked for Snowball everywhere. They called him and hunted for him all over the garden. But he was gone. There wasn't a sign of him anywhere at all.

Susie sat down in the grass and cried loudly. Daniel was very worried too. He did so love Snowball, and it was dreadful not to know where he was. Suppose – just suppose – someone had stolen him and meant to have him for dinner! It was too dreadful to think of.

Daniel didn't dare to tell Susie what he thought, for he knew she would be very unhappy.

Then a strange thing happened and their adventures began. They heard a shrill whistling not far off, very high and strange. The children looked at one another.

'Where does that whistling come from?' asked Susie, drying her eyes.

'It sounds as if it came from the greenhouse,' said Daniel, puzzled. 'But surely it can't, because there's no one there. Let's go and look.'

So they went. The door was open, and they went inside the hot, damp greenhouse. Bright geraniums glowed everywhere, and the maidenhair ferns hung cool and green.

Certainly the whistling came from the greenhouse. The children looked here and there to find what made the noise. And then they found it.

It was made by a small man, who was peeping out of a trapdoor under the staging on which the pots stood. He wore a bright green hat on his head, decorated with red cherries as small as peas. In his mouth was a silver whistle and he was blowing this with all his might.

'I say!' said Daniel in surprise, staring at him. 'Look, Susie! Who's that?'

Susie looked and she couldn't believe her eyes. The man was so tiny, only a little bigger than her biggest doll.

As soon as the little man saw the children looking at him, he took the whistle out of his mouth and beamed at them.

'I thought you'd hear me and come and find out what the noise was,' he said. 'Snowball, your rabbit, gave me a message for you.'

'Snowball gave you a message!' said Daniel, more surprised than ever. 'Where is he?'

'I'll tell you about it,' said the little man, climbing out of the trapdoor and sitting down on an upturned pot nearby. 'Last night the Princess of Nowhere came by in her carriage. It was drawn by four black rabbits, and one of them stepped on a spray of bramble and hurt his foot in your garden. So the coachman hunted about for another rabbit to take his place, and of course he saw Snowball.'

'And did they take Snowball?' asked Susie, her eyes wide open in astonishment.

'Yes,' said the little man. 'He didn't want to go, because it is difficult to get back from the Land of Nowhere, and the Princess Juliana might want to keep him, if he pulled her carriage well. So he was sad to have to go. And he called out a message to me as he went galloping off with the three black rabbits. He said, "Please tell Susie and Daniel where I'm going, and if I'm not back by the time two days and two nights have passed, ask them to come and fetch me."'

'Goodness me!' cried Daniel, hardly able to believe such a strange tale. 'Is it true? Has Snowball really gone to the Land of Nowhere? Where is it?'

'I don't know,' said the little man, shaking his head. 'But if I were you I'd wait till tomorrow night, and then if he isn't back by midnight, I should go and look for him if you love him very much.'

'Yes, we do love him very much,' said Susie. 'But suppose he doesn't come back, how can we find him?'

'I'll help you all I can,' said the little man. 'If he's not back, come and rap on my trapdoor and I'll open it. Come just after midnight.'

'Oh, thank you!' said the two children. 'We will!'

The little man waved goodbye, climbed into the hole and shut the trapdoor down. The children went out of the greenhouse, excited and puzzled. It was all so strange.

They waited all that day and night and all the next day for Snowball. But he didn't come back. They went to bed on the second evening, and kept awake till midnight. Then they crept downstairs to see if Snowball was back in his hutch; but he wasn't.

'Well, we'll have to go and look for him,' said Daniel. 'Are you afraid, Susie?'

'Not a bit,' said Susie. 'I love Snowball too much to

be afraid. Besides, I'll have you to look after me, Daniel.'

'Well, come on, we'll go and rap on the trapdoor,' said Daniel. The moon was shining brightly as they went into the greenhouse. Both children had quickly slipped on their clothes before they had gone down to the garden, just in *case* they might have to go and look for Snowball, so they were quite ready.

The trapdoor was fast closed. Daniel could hardly see where it was. At last he found it and rapped on it. At first nothing happened – and then, when he rapped more loudly a second time, it suddenly flew open and the little man looked out.

'Hallo, hallo, hallo!' he said. 'I was quite expecting you. So Snowball hasn't come back?'

'No,' said Daniel. 'And we're going to look for him and bring him back. You said you'd help us.'

'I can't help you much, I'm afraid,' said the little man. 'But I'll take you to someone who *might* be able to help you a lot. Come down through the trapdoor.'

'We can't,' said Daniel. 'We're too big!'

'Nonsense!' said the little man with a laugh. 'Try and see!'

Daniel put his foot through the trapdoor – and goodness me, what a surprise! He suddenly grew as small as the little man, and found it was quite easy to squeeze through the trapdoor. He looked up at Susie. She seemed enormous and she was gazing at him in the greatest astonishment.

'Come on, Susie!' called Daniel. 'It's all right!'

So Susie put *her* foot into the trapdoor and she too shot down small – as small as one of her dolls. She was so surprised.

'The greenhouse looks enormous!' she said, looking round. 'I say, Daniel, isn't this an adventure!'

'Come on,' said the little man. 'We haven't much time to spare. What are your names? Mine is Squiddle.'

'What a funny name!' said Susie, laughing. 'Mine's Susie, and this is Daniel.'

'What peculiar names!' said Squiddle, laughing

too. 'I've never heard them before – but Squiddle is quite a common name in Fairyland.'

'Are you a fairy then?' asked Daniel, excited.

'Well, not exactly,' said Squiddle. 'I'm half a goblin and half a pixie. But I belong to the fairy folk and know them all. Come along, down this passage, and mind the step at the end.'

Along they all went, and soon came to a big door with a lamp hanging over it. On the door was a brass plate on which a name was written – MR SPECTACLES.

'Mr Spectacles!' said Daniel, laughing. 'Another funny name!'

Squiddle knocked at the door and it opened. A tall, thin man peered out, and Daniel and Susie saw why he had such a peculiar name. He wore three pairs of spectacles! One was at the end of his nose, one was on the bridge of his nose and the third pair was up on his forehead.

'What do you want?' asked Mr Spectacles, in a gruff voice.

'Oh, Mr Spectacles, could you help these two children?' asked Squiddle. 'They want to go to the Land of Nowhere, and they don't know where it is. You know so much, and you have so many clever books to tell you everything you want to know. Could you tell them which way to go?'

'Come in and sit down,' said Mr Spectacles, smiling a sudden smile at the two shy children. 'I'll see what I can do.'

Daniel and Susie sat down in two big armchairs. Squiddle sat down on a stool. The children stared and stared at funny Mr Spectacles and his three pairs of glasses. They longed to know why he wore so many pairs at once.

'I'll help you on one condition,' said Mr Spectacles, putting a fourth pair of spectacles on his nose. 'And that is that you don't ask me why I wear so many pairs of spectacles. I'm so tired of answering that question.'

Daniel and Susie were very glad they hadn't asked it.

'We shouldn't dream of asking you things you didn't want to tell us,' said Daniel politely. 'But please *could* you tell us where the Land of Nowhere is?'

'Well, it might be Anywhere!' said Mr Spectacles. 'Yes, it might be Anywhere!'

'Well, could you tell us where Anywhere is and we'll go and look there,' said Susie.

'Yes, I'll tell you where Anywhere is,' said Mr Spectacles, and he took down a great big atlas with many strange maps in it. He poked his finger here and there and at last pointed to an island in the middle of a yellow sea.

'Anywhere is on the island at the moment,' he said. 'It's a strange land, you know; it moves about from place to place. Well, Nowhere might possibly be in the middle of Anywhere. So I should advise you to look there.'

'How can we get there?' asked Susie.

'Take the train to Golden Sands, and catch the boat to the Island of Anywhere,' said Mr Spectacles, taking off the fourth pair of spectacles and polishing them with his handkerchief. 'But mind you catch the boat – there's only one goes every week, and that's tomorrow.'

'But can we travel all night?' asked Daniel.

'It's daytime in Fairyland, so you'll be all right,' said Mr Spectacles. 'Off you go now, and catch the train. And thanks very much for not asking about my spectacles!'

'I'll go with you,' said Squiddle, taking the children by the hands. 'I'd like to help you.'

So Daniel and Susie and the little man in the green hat went out of the door and into the passage again. Squiddle hurried them up some steps and they suddenly came to what looked like a tiny room with a seat in it. Squiddle pushed the children down on the seat and pulled a rope hanging nearby.

'Oooooooh!' gasped the children – for the little room was a lift and it shot up tremendously quickly, quite taking away their breaths. It rose up for about three minutes and at last came to a stop on a very high hill.

'Get out,' said Squiddle. 'The lift's going down again.'

They walked out of the lift and watched it sink swiftly down into the hill, out of sight. Then they looked round. What a long way they could see! The hill was very, very steep, and as slippery as glass. Nobody could possibly climb up or down it. Just behind them, resting on the shoulders of the hill, was a long bank of cloud. It stayed quite still and didn't move at all, as clouds usually do.

'Where's the train?' asked Susie. 'Surely there can't possibly be a railway on this hill!'

'It's a cloud railway,' explained Squiddle. 'You wait a minute and you'll see the train! It's due very soon.'

Almost as he spoke there came the rattle of wheels, and to the children's great delight they saw the prettiest train imaginable running along the bank of cloud just near them. It was the colour of the blue sky, and each carriage was in the shape of a bird.

'How does it go?' asked Daniel. 'Does it go by steam?'

'No, by lightning,' said Squiddle. 'You'll see how quickly it goes when you're in it.'

They all climbed into a carriage that was shaped like a kingfisher. The engine driver, a goblin with a funny apple-like face, leant out to see that they were safely in, and then off they went, running along the clouds in the sky.

The train went so very fast that both children clutched hold of the sides of the car and had to gasp for breath.

'Oh, goodness!' said Daniel, when at last he could speak. 'It certainly does go like lightning!'

It was a wonderful ride. It was bright daylight, just as Mr Spectacles had said, and the children had a marvellous view of their world as they travelled swiftly along the clouds on the strange, airy railway. Then they came to Fairyland and saw the beautiful spires, towers and pinnacles of that dream-like land.

They wished the journey would never end, as they travelled along the clouds that hung over Fairyland.

'I hope we shall catch the boat to Anywhere,' said Squiddle suddenly, looking anxiously at a very large red watch. 'The train's not so fast as usual. There was a big storm last night and some of the lightning got used up, so there's not so much for the train today.'

'Oh, my, I hope we shall be in time,' said Susie in dismay. 'Mr Spectacles said there was only one boat a week.'

On and on went the train, and at last the children cried out that they could see the sea.

'Then we're nearly there,' said Squiddle, looking at his watch again. 'I hope my watch is fast.'

The train came to a standstill on a cloud that rested on another very high hill. Out jumped Squiddle and the children and rushed to a lift that stood waiting. They got into it, Squiddle pulled the rope and down they shot at such a speed that Susie really thought she was falling and cried out in fright.

The lift stopped at the bottom and the three of them ran out. They found themselves on a beach where the sand was as bright as gold.

'This is Golden Sands,' said Squiddle. 'Oh dear, where's the boat?'

'There it is!' cried Daniel, pointing. 'It's gone!'

Sure enough it had! It was far out to sea, a big boat with yellow sails. 'We're too late,' said Squiddle sadly. 'We're too late. Now what shall we do? Can you possibly wait a week? Then you could catch the next boat.'

'No, we couldn't possibly,' said Daniel. 'Why, our mother would worry terribly if we didn't go home.'

'Oh, we must, we *must* rescue Snowball,' said Susie, with tears in her eyes. 'Oh, Squiddle, can't you think of something?'

Squiddle shook his head. Susie began to cry properly and Daniel and Squiddle took out their handkerchiefs and tried to comfort her. She wouldn't be comforted and she made such a noise that Daniel was quite upset.

'What's the matter with the little girl?' asked a surprised voice suddenly. Daniel looked up and saw a mermaid sitting on a rock, her tail in a warm pool.

'We've missed the boat and don't know how to get to Anywhere,' he said sadly.

'Why don't you fly?' asked the mermaid, beginning to comb out her hair. 'Mother Dibble has a fine lot of gulls' wings to lend to people who miss the boat. She only charges a penny a time.'

'Where does Mother Dibble live?' asked Squiddle.

'In that cave over there,' said the mermaid, pointing. The children turned and saw a cave nearby, with a little gate in front of it.

'Oh, we'll go and get some wings then,' said Squiddle gladly. He took the children's hands and they went over to the cave. Mother Dibble was sitting in it, sewing. All around her hung beautiful wings, grey, white and black.

'Good day, Mother Dibble,' said Squiddle politely. 'Would you lend us three pairs of gulls' wings, please?

We have missed the boat and we want to get to the Island of Anywhere at once. Here are three pennies for the wings.'

Mother Dibble took the pennies, and then chose three pairs of pearly-grey wings. She fastened them carefully to their shoulders. The children felt most excited. They had often flown in dreams, but never in real life, and they could hardly wait until their wings were safely on.

'Spread them out well, and fly slowly,' said Mother Dibble.

They spread their wings and flapped them – and at once they rose up into the air! It was glorious. The children flew strongly over the water, and in a little while they had passed right over the ship they had missed.

'We shall be there before the ship!' cried Daniel. 'Oh, look, Squiddle – is that the Island of Anywhere?'

'Yes,' said Squiddle. 'Isn't it strange?'

It was indeed a strange island, for it changed

its shape as they watched it. It seemed alive. In the centre of it was a shining town, whose towers gleamed like gold.

'Ah, that's the Land of Nowhere,' said Squiddle, pleased. 'Mr Spectacles said it might be Anywhere and so it is! It's in the middle of the island, so we are sure to find your rabbit, Snowball, there. Hurray!'

They all flew down into the shining town. 'We had better go to the palace and ask for the stables,' said Squiddle. So he stopped a hurrying gnome and asked the way to the palace of the Princess Juliana. Then on they went, their big gulls' wings folded neatly behind them.

They came to the glittering palace and walked a little way round it, to where the stables were. Squiddle pushed open a door in the wall and they passed through it into the stables. Rabbits were kept there, all jet black and beautiful. Their whiskers were carefully curled each morning and their ears were brushed. The children couldn't see their white rabbit, Snowball, anywhere.

They asked a servant where he was.

'Oh, the Princess Juliana likes him so much that she has made him her pet,' said the little servant. 'He is sitting on a black velvet cushion by her knee, in the palace.'

'Goodness! Now we shall have to go and ask her for him,' said Squiddle. 'That may be awkward. Listen, children, if the princess is unkind and won't let Snowball go, wait for a signal from me. Then, as soon as you see me wink hard at you, snatch up Snowball and run to the window. Fly out and up into the sky as quickly as you can. I'll stay behind to stop the princess from sending her flying gnomes after you.'

Feeling most excited the children went with Squiddle to the palace gates. They went through them and made their way into the palace. They asked a servant to take them to the princess, and when at last they came to where she was sitting they saw, to their great joy, their lovely rabbit, Snowball, sitting on a cushion at her feet, looking very bored and unhappy.

'Oh, Snowball!' cried Susie joyfully, and she ran to him and hugged him. 'Oh, Your Highness, this is my darling bunny! You borrowed him the other night when one of your rabbits went lame, but now I have come to fetch him home again.'

The Princess Juliana was very beautiful and spoilt. She shook her curly golden head and looked cross.

'He is my pet now,' she said. 'You can't have him. You shall have a sack of gold instead.'

'No, I want my rabbit,' said Susie firmly. The princess cried out crossly and ran to ring a big bell near the fireplace. 'I will tell my servants to turn you out of the palace,' she cried angrily. 'You shan't have Snowball.'

Squiddle winked hard at Susie and Daniel. They knew it was a signal to act at once, so Daniel picked up the rabbit in his arms, and Susie ran to the window and opened it. In a second the children spread out their wings and were up in the air! Squiddle was left behind to stop the princess from sending servants after them.

Over the sea flew Daniel and Susie, leaving the strange Land of Nowhere, set in the Island of Anywhere, far behind them. They wondered if Squiddle was all right – and then, to their great delight, they heard the swish-swish of big wings and there he was, flying beside them once more!

'I couldn't stop the princess from sending out her flying gnomes!' he cried breathlessly. 'We mustn't stop at Golden Sands, for there is no train to take us away. We must fly straight on!'

Daniel and Susie looked behind and saw a whole crowd of little gnomes flying swiftly through the air after them. They flapped their gulls' wings all the faster and soon the gnomes were left behind. On went the children, and on and on, Daniel carrying the frightened rabbit carefully in his arms, and Squiddle keeping a lookout for the gnomes.

'Fly down to earth now,' he said suddenly. So down they flew and landed in a garden – and whatever do you think? It was their very own garden, and there was the greenhouse just nearby! They had flown all the way home! As they dropped downwards the daylight disappeared, and when they stood on the ground, everywhere was dark save for faint, shining moonlight. It was night-time again, as soon as they had left Fairyland behind!

'Put Snowball into his hutch and get back to bed quickly,' said Squiddle to the children. 'You'll still be able to get a little sleep. Leave your gulls' wings in the garden. They will fly back to Mother Dibble by themselves.'

Daniel put Snowball safely back into his hutch. Then the children said a loving goodnight to him, and you should have seen how his nose twitched with delight to be safely home again! Then they carefully took off their wings and put them on the grass. Just as they turned to go indoors they heard a swishing sound – and hey presto, the wings rose up by themselves and flew away! It was very strange.

'Goodbye, goodbye,' whispered Squiddle, pressing

their hands. 'I'm glad I was able to help you. Come and see me again sometimes.'

'Oh, we will!' said the children. 'Goodbye and thank you so much!'

They crept into bed, surprised to find themselves their own size once more.

'What an adventure, Susie!' said Daniel, as he put his head down on his pillow. 'It's all mixed up in my mind – the cross princess, the Island of Anywhere, Mother Dibble and the mermaid, the cloud railway and that funny old Mr Spectacles!'

'I *wish* we knew why he wore so many spectacles!' sighed Susie. 'That's just one thing I really *would* like to know!'

I'd like to know too, wouldn't you? But I don't expect we shall ever find out!

The Train that Broke in Half

The Train that Broke
in Half

BENNY WAS a funny little boy. He thought he couldn't do anything well! He was always afraid of things, so he was shy and timid, and hadn't any friends.

'Benny, why don't *you* go in for the races?' his mother said each summer when the school sports day came. But Benny shook his head.

'No, I'm not good at running,' he said. 'I'd only be last, and look silly, Mother.'

'Benny, why don't you ask to belong to the Cub Scouts?' said his father when the spring came and the Scouts and Cubs put on their uniforms and went to have some fun in the fields.

'I'd be no good,' said Benny. 'I'd never learn enough. You have to know a lot.'

'Well, you could learn, as the others do,' said his father. But no, Benny wouldn't try. He was afraid of looking silly and of being laughed at.

It was the same with everything. When he went to parties Benny wouldn't play Musical Chairs because he felt sure he would be the first one out. At Christmas time he wouldn't pull a cracker because he didn't like the bang.

'But, Benny, you've never pulled a cracker in your life, so how do you know you won't like the bang?' asked his mother. 'You may love it, as the other children do. Don't be such a little coward.'

Well, that was quite the wrong thing to say to shy Benny. He at once thought he *was* a little coward, so he became more ashamed and shy than ever. He thought that everyone must think him a coward, so he wouldn't play games in case he fell down and cried, and he wouldn't go to any parties at all.

It was dreadful. His mother didn't know what to do with such a funny boy. The other children got tired of asking him to play with them and left him quite alone. So Benny played by himself all day long, and hardly opened his mouth at school. And yet, secretly, Benny longed to have friends and to shout and run and play. Poor Benny!

Now, not far from Benny's house ran a railway line, deep down in a cutting. Benny loved to watch the trains that ran by. He liked to hear them hooting as they raced past. He knew every one of them, and would have liked to wave to the engine driver, but he was much too shy.

One day he was sitting on the fence, watching the trains, when the long train from the nearest big city came by. It was a corridor train, so that the carriages were closely joined together for people to walk all up and down the train if they wanted to. Benny liked that sort of train, because he could see the people sitting at the dining tables and having their dinner, and he could see people standing in the corridors and looking out of the windows.

With a loud hoot the train came along, deep down in the cutting. Benny looked at his watch. The train was late, and it was hurrying. Not more than ten minutes behind it would come the next train.

'You'd better hurry!' said Benny to the train. He wouldn't talk to other children, but he often talked to animals and trains and cars. The train hooted and went on.

And then a strange thing happened. The three last carriages of the train suddenly broke away and got left behind!

Benny stared as if he couldn't believe his eyes! The rest of the train went rushing on, and was soon out of sight. Just those three carriages were left behind. They ran a little way, and then stopped on the line.

'It's broken in half,' said Benny to himself. 'The train's broken in half! Where's the guard?

Will he pop his head out of the guard's van and see what's happened?'

But no guard popped his head out. He couldn't because he was in the other part of the train. He had gone to speak to the ticket collector who happened to be on the train – so he didn't know anything about his van being left behind.

Nobody was in the last three carriages at all. They were quite empty. There they stood on the line, looking rather silly.

Benny soon saw that there was nobody in them. He stared and stared – and then had a dreadful thought.

What about the next train that would come rushing along in a few minutes' time? It wouldn't know those carriages were left on the line. Nobody knew but Benny. The signalman didn't know. The engine driver wouldn't know – and he would go crashing into them!

'Then there would be an accident,' said Benny. 'Oh dear! Whatever shall I do?'

For once Benny forgot that he thought himself a poor little coward, no good at anything. He only thought of the people in the train that was soon coming into that deep railway cutting, and would crash into the carriages there. Benny sprang down from the fence. *If I run for all I'm worth, I could perhaps get to the signal box in time, and tell the man to change the signal to red!* thought the little boy. *That would stop it!*

He began to run. Benny hadn't thought he was any good at running at all – but how he ran now! His legs twinkled in and out, and his breath came in big pants. His chest felt as if it would burst, but Benny didn't care. No, he must, he must, he *must* get to that signal box in time!

It was quite a long way – but at last Benny saw it in the distance. His legs were so tired that they could hardly run, but he made them go on and on until he reached the signal box. The signalman was leaning out of his box, and he saw Benny.

Now in the ordinary way Benny wouldn't have

dared to speak to a signalman – but now he didn't care what he did. He could hear the train coming!

He turned his head, and there it was, rushing along the line – the train that would crash into the three carriages! Benny tried to shout, but his voice was so full of puffs and pants that he could hardly get his words out.

'Signalman, change the signal to red!' he panted. 'There are some carriages left on the line – broken off the last train!'

The signalman could hardly understand the breathless boy, but he at once pulled a heavy lever – and to Benny's great delight the signal that had been green for the train to pass by changed to red, just as the train came rumbling up at great speed.

The driver saw the signal change to red and he put on his brakes very suddenly. With a long screech the train slowed down and then stopped. Passengers popped their heads out of the windows to see what was the matter.

Benny got back his breath. He yelled to the signalman, 'The last train broke in half! It left three carriages behind up the line. I only just got there in time to warn you.'

'Good for you, young man!' said the signalman. He ran down from his box and went to the engine driver. Then the train went slowly on, taking the signalman too, and soon everyone saw the three left-behind carriages.

'That was a narrow escape,' said the engine driver, looking pale. 'I'd have been right into those carriages if you hadn't put the signal against me.'

'It's that boy who saved the train,' said the signalman, looking round for Benny. But Benny was gone! You won't believe it, but all his shyness and fear came back again when he saw so many passengers looking at him. He ran home quickly and went into his bedroom. He was trembling now. He couldn't think how he could have done such a thing!

That teatime his mother was full of the whole

affair. 'Fancy, Benny,' she said, 'a boy saved the London train! He saw some carriages left behind on the line, and he tore to the signalman to tell him – and the next train was saved. Oh, Benny, if only you could do a thing like that! How proud Daddy and I would be of you!'

Benny looked at his mother. He knew how often he had disappointed her because he had been so silly and shy and afraid. Now he had a big surprise in store for her!

'Would you really be proud of me?' he said. 'I'd like that, Mother!'

'Oh, Benny, I'd be so proud I'd run out and tell everyone about you!' said his mother. 'But you're such a funny little quiet boy – you'd never do anything wonderful, you'd be too scared!'

Just then a knock came at the door – and who should be there but the signalman! He knew Benny and knew where he lived – and he had come to say a few words to him. And behind him was a crowd of children – the boys and girls of Benny's school, who had already heard about Benny from the signalman!

'Where's Benny?' said the signalman. 'Ah, there you are! You're a hero, Benny! You saved the train! My goodness, I saw you running to my box, and I've never seen anyone run so fast in my life! Never! You'd win any race if you ran like that. I want to shake hands with you.'

And he solemnly shook hands with Benny, while Benny's mother and father looked on in the greatest surprise.

'But was it our *Benny* who saved the train?' cried his father. 'Good gracious! To think Benny could do that! Benny, Benny, I'm proud of you! I always thought you were a timid little fellow – but my word, you're a hero!'

His mother hugged him. His father clapped him on the back. The signalman shook his hand up and down – and in crowded all the boys and girls, yelling, 'Benny, Benny! Tell us all about it. Come out, Benny, we want to see you.'

And then, all of a sudden, Benny was a hero. He didn't feel a cowardly little fellow any more. He wasn't afraid of anything. He wanted to shout and run and climb. He was changed from top to toe!

'I didn't know I could do it – but I did!' he kept telling himself. 'I was wrong about myself. I was silly and shy just because I thought myself to be silly and shy – but I'm not really. I'm brave and bold – I can run very fast. I can do great things! Oh, I'm glad, I'm glad! Everything will be different now!'

And so it is – for Benny himself is different, you see. The passengers of the train collected money to give to the boy who saved them, and they bought Benny a fine toy motor car, which he drives down the streets every day. And to hear him come hooting along at a fine pace, you'd never think he was once a poor, shy little fellow who couldn't say boo to a goose!

You never know what you can do until you try!

Belinda All Alone

Belinda All Alone

MOLLIE HAD been playing in the garden with her teddy bear and her doll. She took them right down to the bottom where the wall was, and played with them there. She climbed into the old pear tree and sat on a smooth branch, pulling the teddy up beside her, but she put Belinda, the doll, on the top of the wall.

'You might get your clean clothes dirty if you sit in the tree,' she said. 'Teddy hasn't any clothes to get dirty.'

Just as she was swinging Teddy up and down on the branch her mother called her.

'Mollie! Here is Auntie Juliet come to see you!'

Mollie jumped down from the tree in excitement for she loved her Auntie Juliet. She took Teddy with her but she forgot all about poor Belinda, who was left sitting on the top of the wall all by herself.

And, oh dear me, Mollie didn't think of poor Belinda again that day! She forgot all about her, and not even when she put her toys away and went to bed did she think of Belinda sitting all alone on the top of the garden wall.

But the toys in the toy cupboard missed her.

'Where is Belinda?' asked the panda, looking all round.

'Oh! She must still be on the garden wall,' said the teddy bear, remembering. 'Mollie left her there when she ran to see her Aunt Juliet. She took me with her, but she left Belinda behind.'

'Good gracious!' said the clown doll in surprise. 'Poor old Belinda! She will be dreadfully cold and frightened sitting there by herself all night. And supposing she fell off. She might break her leg.'

The toys looked at one another in dismay. They all liked Belinda, who was very cheerful and merry, and they couldn't bear to think of her lonely and cold.

'Shall we go and fetch her?' asked the teddy, after a while. 'I don't mind going, if someone else will come with me.'

'It's so dark,' said the clown, looking out of the window.

'I'd be afraid something would catch me and eat me,' said the wooden soldier, shivering.

'Well, something might catch and eat Belinda!' said the teddy. 'That would be dreadful. Come on, somebody! Who will go with me?'

'I will,' said a small voice.

Everyone looked to see who it was. It was the little clockwork mouse! He was a very timid creature, but Belinda had once stroked him and he had never forgotten it.

'All right,' said the teddy. 'Come on.'

'Wind me up first,' said the tiny mouse. 'I can't go unless I'm wound up.'

So the clown wound him up and he and the teddy bear started out together. They crept out of the window and slid down the drainpipe outside. The little mouse landed on his nose, but he said he wasn't hurt so they went on again.

It was dark – very dark! The teddy walked straight into a flower tub and bumped his head hard. The little mouse rubbed the bump for him and then they went on once more.

Suddenly a great creature pushed by them, and Teddy felt a sharp prick.

'Ooh! Something has stabbed me!' he cried. 'It's an enemy with a sword!'

The mouse squeaked in dismay, and the big creature stopped. They could just see its eyes glinting.

'I shan't hurt you,' it said. 'I'm only a harmless hedgehog, hunting for beetles. You haven't seen any, I suppose?'

'No,' said the teddy bear. 'I say, what did you stab me with?'

'Oh, one of my prickles must have pricked you,' said the hedgehog. 'I'm very sorry. Well, if you see any beetles, send them my way, please!'

Off it went again, and the teddy bear started on his way once more. But the little mouse called to him, 'Teddy! You'll have to wind me up again. I've run down!'

So Teddy wound him up and then he ran beside him on his little wheels. They went on towards the bottom of the garden, and, oh my, whatever was this that suddenly swooped down on them? It picked the clockwork mouse up in its claws, but Teddy caught hold of him and shouted loudly, 'Let go, let go!'

'Hallo, who are you?' said a surprised voice. 'I am a brown owl.'

'I'm a teddy bear,' said the teddy. 'Please let my friend go. He's not a real mouse, only a clockwork one.'

'Is that so?' said the owl, and his big, round eyes

looked closely at the frightened little mouse. 'So he is! Well, I don't like the taste of clockwork mice, so I'll let him go. I'm hunting real mice. If you meet any, send them my way, will you?'

He flew up into the air with a soft, feathery sound and the two toys went on their way once more. The teddy trod on a slug and slipped over, and the mouse ran into a big snail and had to be wound up again, but they had no more adventures before they reached the garden wall.

'Belinda! Belinda! Are you there?' called the teddy.

'Oh, Teddy, is it you?' came Belinda's little voice. 'Oh, I'm so frightened! There's a great big face looking at me over this wall, and I'm dreadfully afraid. Have you come to rescue me?'

'Yes, and the clockwork mouse is with me,' said the teddy bear. 'I'll climb up the pear tree and come and fetch you. The mouse can keep guard at the bottom.'

Belinda heard the teddy climbing up the pear tree

and soon he was beside her. He put his arm round her and hugged her.

'Don't be frightened any more,' he said. 'We'll take you home safely.'

'Look at that great shining face staring at us through those trees,' whispered Belinda. 'I'm so frightened of it. Do you think it will eat us?'

'I hope not,' said the teddy, looking at the big round face and shivering all down his back. 'Come on quickly while there's time!'

He helped Belinda down the tree, and they soon came to where the clockwork mouse was waiting.

'Wind me up again,' he said. 'I've run down.'

But, oh dear me, something had gone wrong with his clockwork and the key seemed dreadfully stiff. It took ages and ages to wind him. And all of a sudden Belinda gave a shriek and pointed upwards.

'There's that horrid face looking at us again!' she said. Sure enough it was! It was peeping over the wall now, and the teddy bear didn't like it a bit.

'We must run!' he said. 'Come on, mouse, you're wound up enough now. Take my hand, Belinda.'

They hurried up the garden, and except for once when the mouse fell into a puddle and had to be wound up to get out of it, nothing happened. They scrambled up the drainpipe and fell into the room, frightened and out of breath.

'What's the hurry?' asked the clown in surprise. 'Is anything after you?'

'Yes, something with a great, big, shining face!' said the teddy. 'Ooh, look! It's peeping in at the window!'

Then the clown laughed till the tears, ran down his face.

'You sillies!' he cried. 'It's only the moon! Fancy being frightened of the moon!'

And sure enough, it was! Teddy did feel silly, but he didn't mind a bit when Belinda kissed him and said he and the clockwork mouse were the bravest of all the toys in the toy cupboard.

'Clown may laugh at you now,' she said, 'but he

wasn't brave enough to come out in the night and rescue me! You and I and the clockwork mouse will always be friends now, won't we?'

And they are. If you look into Mollie's toy cupboard any morning you will see them there, close together – Belinda, the teddy bear and the little clockwork mouse!

Granny's Lovely Necklace

Granny's Lovely Necklace

GRANNY, MUMMY, Daddy, Eileen and Jim were all down by the sea. It was such fun! The weather was fine and sunny, the sea was blue and the sands were smooth and yellow.

Granny was very happy. She did like being with everyone she loved. Eileen and Jim were very kind to her, because really she was the sweetest old lady you could imagine. She was always diving into her big bag for sweets, or cakes, or apples for Eileen and Jim, and she was always ready to listen to all they said or to tell them stories about the exciting things she did when she was a little girl.

Granny had a lovely necklace which she nearly always wore. It was made of shiny crystal beads with pretty blue ones here and there. Mummy and Daddy had given it to her for a birthday present, and Granny was very proud of it. Once she let Eileen wear it for a whole afternoon, and Eileen felt as grand as could be.

One day Granny lost her necklace. She simply couldn't *think* where it had gone. She felt for it round her neck – and it wasn't there!

'Oh dear, oh dear!' she said in alarm. 'My necklace is lost! Eileen! Jim! Tell me, can you see my lovely necklace round my neck or anywhere on me at all?'

Eileen and Jim looked – but there was no shining necklace to be seen.

'Granny, it must have dropped off your neck when we went out in the boat this morning,' said Jim suddenly. 'You know, I thought I heard something fall into the water, and I thought it was my knife – but it must have been your necklace. I felt for my knife, and it was safely in my pocket.'

'Oh dear, do you really think it fell into the sea?' said poor Granny. 'Well, it's lost for good then. I shall never find it again. I am so sad about it.'

Granny looked so unhappy that Eileen and Jim felt unhappy too. They knew how horrid it was to lose anything they really liked. Once Jim had lost his favourite blue pencil and once Eileen had lost her second best doll – and they had both worried all day long.

Mummy and Daddy were told about the necklace. They were very sorry too.

'You had it on when you got into the boat this morning with the children,' said Mummy. 'I remember seeing it flash in the sun. Yes, Granny dear – you must have dropped it overboard when you leant over to look at the fish or something.'

'Well, it's gone now,' said Granny. 'I must just put up with it.'

That afternoon Jim and Eileen were to go off for a picnic with Mummy, and they were going to leave

Daddy to play golf and Granny to read by herself. But somehow the children didn't like going off to enjoy themselves when Granny was feeling rather upset.

'Let's put off the picnic till tomorrow,' said Jim to Eileen. 'We'll get out our big shrimping net and we'll go shrimping to see if we can catch lots of shrimps for Granny's tea. You know how she loves shrimps. That will be a treat for her to make up for her lost necklace.'

'That's a good idea, Jim,' said Eileen. 'I'll fetch the net. I know where it is.'

Jim told Mummy about his idea. Mummy was pleased because she thought it was kind of the children. 'Granny won't be alone for tea if we don't go for a picnic,' she said. 'And *won't* she be pleased to have a feast of shrimps!'

Eileen and Jim went off with their net. The tide was coming in. 'It will bring the shrimps with it!' said Jim. 'I do hope there will be lots of big ones.'

They took off their shoes and stockings and ran to the edge of the water. They had seen the fisher-girls with their enormous nets shrimping at a certain place on the beach, and they guessed that was good for shrimps. They began to push the net lightly over the surface of the sand, a little way in the water.

'You can have a turn first, Eileen,' said Jim. 'I'll carry the basket.'

So Eileen went first. The little waves curled round her legs. They were warm and tickly. Eileen liked to feel them. She pushed the net along, hoping there would be lots of shrimps in it when she looked.

'Have a look now,' said Jim. So Eileen lifted up the net carefully.

'Oooh! Oooh! Look at them jumping!' cried Jim in delight. 'You *have* caught a nice lot, Eileen! Let's put them into the basket.'

They put them into the basket. There were eleven! Six of them were so big that they really almost looked like prawns.

'Now your turn, Jim,' said Eileen. She gave him the shrimping net, and took the basket. Jim pushed the net along the sand eagerly. It was such fun to shrimp. He did hope he would catch as many shrimps as Eileen.

'I'll look and see how many I've got now,' he said at last. He lifted up the net – but will you believe it, there was only one tiny green crab in the net! Not a single shrimp jumped there! Jim was so disappointed.

'Have another turn, Jim,' said Eileen generously. But Jim shook his head.

'No,' he said, 'it's your turn, Eileen. I've had mine. I'll have another in a minute.'

So Eileen had a second turn – and do you know, when she lifted up the net again she had fourteen shrimps! They were nearly all big ones. She could hardly believe her eyes.

'I really am lucky,' she said to Jim, as they emptied the shrimps into the basket. 'Now your turn again, Jim.'

Poor old Jim! He didn't catch any shrimps when he had his second turn either, and not even a crab – only a big piece of seaweed. He was dreadfully disappointed.

He couldn't think why he was so unlucky.

'Perhaps you push the net too deeply into the sand and frighten away the shrimps before they get into the net,' said Eileen. 'I'll have my third turn now. I wonder if I'll catch any more!'

Eileen was certainly lucky that afternoon. She caught forty-three shrimps altogether, though poor Jim didn't catch one. But he caught something much better. Listen!

He was having his last turn. He lifted up the net to see if he had got a shrimp *this* time – and he saw something glittering in the net. Whatever do you think he had caught? Guess!

He had caught Granny's beautiful necklace! What do you think of that? The tide had brought it in to shore and it was lying half-buried in the sand at the edge of the waves. Jim had shrimped just there – and the necklace had slid into his net.

'Eileen! Eileen! Look, I've got Granny's necklace!' shouted Jim in great excitement. 'Oh, do look!'

'Jim! Oh, how lovely! What a surprise! Whatever will Granny say!' cried Eileen in delight. 'Quick! Let's go and tell Mummy.'

So off they ran. Mummy was simply delighted. 'I know what we'll do,' she said. 'I'll cook the shrimps for tea and we'll put them into a covered dish, and we'll wash the necklace and put that into a covered dish too – and we'll tell Granny that you've each caught her something for tea! Won't she be excited!'

So at teatime there were two covered dishes on the table.

'I caught you what's in *that* one!' said Eileen.

Granny opened the first dish. It was full of delicious shrimps.

'Oh, how lovely!' she cried. 'What *can* be in the other dish?'

She took the cover off – and when she saw her lovely necklace glittering there, she could hardly believe her eyes!

'My necklace!' she said joyfully. 'Oh, my lovely

necklace! Children, do please tell me how you found it.'

So they told her how they had given up their picnic to catch her some shrimps for tea, and how Eileen had caught her such a lot of shrimps – and Jim none – and then how he had caught the glittering necklace!

'You are two good, kind children,' said Granny, hugging them both. 'You have given me two beautiful surprises, and now it is my turn to give *you* one! I shall buy Jim that steamer he wanted so much yesterday – and I shall buy Eileen a new spade because hers has a broken handle.'

'Oh, Granny, Granny, it was a good thing after all that you lost your necklace!' cried the children. 'You have got a feast of shrimps – and we shall have new toys!'

'And I have seen how kind my two children can be,' said Mummy, smiling. 'So we are all happy.'

Granny had a new clasp put on her necklace, and she still has it. She told me this story to tell to you. I do hope you like it!

Cowardy Custard

Cowardy Custard

ONCE UPON a time there was a little boy called Charlie. He was eight years old, but he was small for his age. When the other boys played rough games he stood in a corner, afraid of being knocked over. They laughed at him, and pointed at him when he ran away. 'Cowardy, cowardy custard!' they called. 'Look at him, poor little Charlie, afraid of playing games in case he falls over! Poor little cowardy custard!'

Poor Charlie! He did wish he were bigger and stronger so that he could join in the games and not fall over as soon as he was pushed. But his mother and father could not always afford to give him good meals, so the boy didn't grow as strong as he should. His father was a boatman on the river and the summer had been rainy so people had not always wanted boats. Sometimes there was not enough money to buy Charlie good meals when he needed them.

'Come on, Charlie!' cried the boys one day. 'We are going picnicking. Come with us!'

Charlie went – but dear me, how he wished he hadn't when he saw that the boys wanted to climb trees to see who could go the highest! Up they went, as strong as little tigers, and Charlie stayed trembling on the ground below.

His arms were thin and weak, and he thought he would fall if he tried to climb a tree. He was afraid that he would break his leg and then he knew his mother would be very upset.

'Come on, Charlie, climb up!' called the boys. But he wouldn't. He tried to slip away when they were not looking, but they saw him and shouted after him.

'Cowardy, cowardy custard!' they called. 'Cowardy

Charlie, he daren't climb a tree!'

Charlie went red and ran off as quickly as he could. It was dreadful to be called a coward. If only he had been as strong as the other boys he would have been up a tree in a trice! He was sure he wasn't really a coward.

He felt very unhappy. He knew that all the other children in the school would know the next day that he had been afraid to climb a tree and he would be teased more than ever.

At bedtime Charlie lay on his back trying to go to sleep but he couldn't. It was dark outside, and the wind blew down the chimney. It was very late but still Charlie lay wide awake.

The church clock struck twelve. Charlie counted the strokes. He had heard his mother and father going to bed a long time ago. How late it was! The time went slowly on and the little boy heard the clock strike one o'clock. It sounded so loud in the middle of the night.

Then Charlie heard another sound. It seemed like a

long, long howl. Charlie lay and listened. Whatever could it be? The sound came again – a long, drawn-out moan. Charlie sat up in bed. Was it a dog? He listened. The noise came again.

It must be a dog! But why was it making that dreadful noise? Where could it be?

Charlie jumped out of bed and ran downstairs. He opened the front door and looked out at the black river that flowed past the house. He couldn't see it save for a ripple here and there that shone out in the dark night. He could hear the water lapping against the edge. Then the howl came again.

It's a dog howling in the middle of the river! thought Charlie suddenly. *Yes, it is! It has tried to swim across and it can't. Perhaps it is drowning.*

He stood there wondering what to do. He must act quickly or the dog would sink. Oh, how dark and cold the night was! Was he brave enough to find his father's boat, undo the rope and row all by himself on the dark river to find a dog he couldn't see?

Yes, he was. Without stopping to think, Charlie made his way in the darkness to the mooring where his father's boat was tied up, and undid the rope. He stepped into the boat and took up the oars. He began to row over the dark water.

The dog howled again. Charlie called out to it. 'All right, old boy! I'm coming! Keep up till I get to you. Where are you?'

The dog heard and gave a little howl in reply. Charlie listened. It must be right in the middle of the river where the current was strongest. He rowed hard. The dark night was all round him, and he was quite alone – but he didn't feel afraid. He just wanted to get to the dog.

Nearer and nearer he rowed. Then he heard a splashing noise and the dog yelped. Charlie was almost there.

'I'm coming!' he called. 'I'm coming!'

At last he reached the poor animal. It was so tired out that it could not climb into the boat, but was just about to sink. Charlie took hold of it by the collar and hauled it in. It fell down in the bottom of the boat and didn't move. It was too exhausted. The little boy turned the boat round and rowed back through the darkness. He tied the boat to the post and carried the cold, wet dog indoors.

He lit a lamp and looked at it. It was a fox terrier. It lay on the kitchen floor and didn't move. Charlie warmed some milk and poured it into a bowl. The dog lapped it up and let Charlie rub it dry with a towel. Then the boy put it gently on an old rug by the stove and left it to sleep.

Next day his father found out that the dog was a valuable fox terrier belonging to Sir William Brown. He took it back to its owner while Charlie went to school. Poor Charlie! He forgot all about the dog when he reached school for he was so afraid of being teased because he hadn't dared to climb trees the day before.

But before playtime came, the headmaster called

all the boys to him, and spoke to them.

'I have something very pleasant to say to you today,' he said. 'It has come to my attention that one of my boys did a very brave deed last night, and saved the life of a valuable dog belonging to Sir William Brown. This boy heard a dog howling in the middle of the night, and got up and rowed to the middle of the river where the dog was sinking. He saved the dog and today it is safely back with its owner.'

Everyone cheered and wondered who the brave boy could be. Nobody noticed that Charlie had gone as red as a beetroot.

'Now,' said the headmaster, 'Sir William Brown has asked me to say that as this dog is worth a hundred pounds, he wishes to reward the brave boy who rescued it for him. He has sent me five pounds to give him in front of the whole school – and I am very pleased to know that a boy of mine deserves such a fine reward. Charlie Green, come out and collect your reward.'

Charlie stood up, still blushing. All his companions

stared at him with open mouths. What! Could old cowardy custard Charlie really be the boy who had done such a brave deed in the middle of a cold, dark night? He didn't even dare to climb a tree! But he couldn't be a coward if he had done all that the headmaster had said. He must be quite a hero!

The boys began to cheer.

'Hip-hip-hurrah for Charlie! Good old Charlie! Three cheers for Charlie!' they shouted. Charlie walked up to the platform and took the envelope his headmaster gave him.

'I'm proud of you, my boy,' said the headmaster, and shook him by the hand. Charlie was so pleased. He wondered what his mother would say when he reached home and gave her so much money. What a lot of things she could buy!

Nobody teased him at playtime about not climbing trees. Everybody wanted to be with him and talk to him. He was the hero of the day. He was good old Charlie who had saved a dog from drowning in the middle of the night!

And when Charlie reached home that day, eager to give his mother the money in his envelope, there was more good news for him. Sir William had asked his father to go and live on his estate and care for the two big lakes he had there. He would get good wages, a nice house to live in and they would no longer be short of money.

'You shall have plenty of good food and milk,' said his mother. 'You won't be a thin little scarecrow that can't climb trees or run as fast as the others, Charlie. You'll grow into a great big boy and I shall always be proud of you.'

Well, you should see Charlie now! He is bigger than any of the other boys, and as for climbing trees, why, he beats everyone else at that game! And who do you think is his best friend? The little fox terrier he saved one night from drowning! They think the world of one another and I don't wonder at it, do you?

Good Gracious Me!

Good Gracious Me!

IT ALL happened in such a hurry! Leslie was going along the path in the wood on his bicycle, thinking of what he would spend his pocket money on. He was wishing he could save up enough money to buy a bell to put on the handlebar of his bicycle.

Sometimes I go almost as fast as a car, and I really ought to have a bell to warn people to get out of the way! thought Leslie.

Just then somebody rushed by him, almost knocking him over. Leslie was cross. 'Hi! Don't go rushing about like that!' he shouted. Then he stared in surprise.

The person who had nearly knocked him over was the longest-legged man he had ever seen! Leslie stared after him. He had long spidery legs, long arms and a long neck on which sat a big head with pointed ears!

'He must be a gnome or a pixie or something!' said Leslie. And just as he was thinking that, he heard shouts behind him. 'Stop him! Stop, thief! Hi, can't you stop him?'

Then two or three very small men rushed all round Leslie. He thought they must be goblins. They looked very cross and impatient.

'Why don't you stop him? Didn't you see Long-Legs rushing by? He's taken a bag of magic spells from us!'

'Oh,' said Leslie in surprise. 'Well, I didn't know that. Anyway, he's gone. You'll never catch him, he's got such long legs!'

'Lend us your bicycle!' said one of the goblins, and caught hold of it. 'Come on! Lend it to us! We can go fast on this.'

'No,' said Leslie, who felt sure he would never see

his nice new bicycle again if he let the little men have it.

'Yes!' said the little men, and they all jumped on the bicycle at once, with Leslie in the middle of them, and then they made Leslie pedal very quickly. The bicycle simply shot through the trees!

'Let me slow down! We'll have an accident!' said Leslie. But he might as well have spoken to the moon. The little men shouted at him to pedal faster and faster. They held on to Leslie and to each other; it must have been a funny sight to see them tearing along at top speed through the wood!

'There he is! Go on, faster, faster!' yelled the little man who was right in front.

And faster they went, till Leslie could hardly breathe! Then crash! They bumped into a tree and all of them fell off. The front wheel of the bicycle looked a little bent. But the little men took no notice of that! No, up they all jumped again, nearly leaving poor Leslie behind this time, and off they went once more, with Leslie clinging to the handlebars for all he was worth.

'I can see him! I can see Long-Legs!' yelled the front goblin. 'He's going to the goblin market. That's where he's going. He means to sell our spells there. Hurry!'

They left the path in the wood and came out on a main road. Leslie knew he had never been there before. It was crowded with all kinds of fairy folk! How he stared!

'We shall knock people over. Look out!' he shouted. 'I'm going too fast.'

'Ring your bell then, ring it, ring it!' yelled the little men.

'I haven't got one!' said Leslie. 'I must slow down. I nearly knocked over that pixie.'

'We'd better stop and buy a bell,' said the little man at the front. 'We don't want an accident.'

So they stopped at a shop and bought a most wonderful bell. It looked like silver to Leslie, and how it shone! They fixed it on to the handlebar.

Then on they tore again, this time ringing for all they were worth. Ting-a-ling! Ting-a-ling! Ting-a-ling!

People hopped out of the way at once. The bicycle raced on as fast as an express train. Leslie couldn't help enjoying it, especially as he was the one to ring the bell!

'There's Long-Legs again!' yelled the little men. 'Faster, faster!'

Ting-a-ling! Ting-a-ling! On they went and, just as they reached the crowded market, they caught up with Long-Legs. In fact they ran right into him, and knocked him over! Everyone fell off the bicycle, and then the goblins swarmed over the groaning Long-Legs like ants. They took away his bag of spells and tied his hands behind him, and began to march him away.

'Hi!' called Leslie. 'Tell me the way home!'

The goblins stopped. They seemed to have forgotten about Leslie. 'Oh, don't you know it?' they called. 'Well, never mind, your bicycle does. Just hop on and it will take you back to the path in the wood.' Leslie was rather doubtful about this. He hadn't noticed that his bicycle was very clever before.

'Well, what about your bell?' he called. 'Don't you want it?'

'Oh, no. You can have it in return for letting us borrow your bicycle,' called back the goblins. 'Goodbye.'

'Goodbye,' said Leslie, and looked at his new bell in delight. Goodness, what would his mother say?

He got on his bicycle and pushed off. To his surprise and delight it raced along by itself, and he didn't even need to pedal again until he reached the path that he knew, in the middle of the wood.

There was no one about, of course, but Leslie couldn't help ringing his bell. Ting-a-ling! Ting-a-ling! And all the rabbits scuttled out of the way at once.

He got home at last, feeling quite tired. When he told his mother how he got his new bell, she didn't believe him.

'All right, I'll take you to the market and you'll see all I saw!'

But isn't it a pity – he can't find the way again now. Still, perhaps he will some day.

Quite an Adventure

Quite an Adventure

'LEND ME your boat when you go fishing, Alan,' begged Geoffrey. 'Go on – I lent you my floating bed yesterday. I'll look after your ship all right.'

'You won't!' said Alan. 'You'll let it go loose, just for the fun of it – and the tide will take it away. I know you!'

'I tell you I'll look after it,' said Geoffrey. 'You know I will. You're just being selfish – won't lend anyone anything!'

'Now you're being a fat-head,' said Alan. 'All right, I *will* lend you my ship, but just remember this – it's a beautiful handmade one, and my grandfather gave it to me for my birthday, and it's very valuable because it was his as a boy, and it's as old as the hills! You don't get ships like that now.'

'I know,' said Geoffrey. 'And I do promise to be careful. Thanks most awfully, Alan.'

That afternoon, when Alan went swimming in the bay with his friends, Geoffrey took the beautiful ship down to the waves. It was quite heavy, and so beautifully made that everyone stared at it as he passed. It could sail wonderfully well too, and took the wind just like a real ship.

Geoffrey waded out a good way, and then set the boat carefully down on the water. It seemed to come alive at once, and rode the waves marvellously. Geoffrey held the long string as loosely as he could, so that the ship could feel as if it were sailing on its own.

'Lovely ship, good ship, sturdy ship!' said Geoffrey, watching it with pride. 'You're as beautiful as a white-winged gull! You look as if you might spread your sails in the air and fly away on the wind!'

Geoffrey waded out further, where the waves swelled up high. If the ship wanted to go on deep water, it should! And then, quite suddenly, there came a really enormous wave, towering up over Geoffrey! It broke over him, and he lost his footing and went under the water, gasping. He could only swim a little, but fortunately his feet felt the bottom again at once, and his head popped safely out of the water.

'Whew!' said Geoffrey, spitting out saltwater. 'What a wave! Oh, I say – the string's slipped out of my fingers. The ship, the ship – where is it?'

There it was, a little way out, bobbing proudly up and down on the waves. Geoffrey stared at it. It was sailing over deep water now – and he couldn't *really* swim. Just a few strokes wouldn't be enough to get to the boat, and bring it back. He might be drowned if a wave knocked him over again.

But that boat – that precious boat! What *would* Alan say if he came back, and found it gone – gone far out to sea, never to come back again?

But I can't wade out in that deep water and get it, I can't, thought poor Geoffrey, almost in tears. *Oh,* I *know what I can do! I'll wade back to shore and get my rubber floating bed and my spade, and I'll paddle the bed out after the ship! I could catch it up then, I'm sure I could!*

So back to the shore he waded, and ran to where he had left his rubber floating bed. It was well blown up, thank goodness. Geoffrey carried it down to the sea, his spade over his shoulder. He laid the bed down on the waves and slid himself on to it. He sat there, with his spade in his hand, trying to see where the ship had gone to.

'There it is! It's not so *very* far out!' he said joyfully. 'I can soon reach it if I paddle hard with my spade.'

He dipped the spade in the water, and was soon paddling hard with it. Swish-swish it went, swish-swish, and the rubber bed shot over the waves, going up and down with them. It was really most exciting.

But the ship still seemed quite far away. *Of course –*

the tide's going out – and taking the ship with it! thought Geoffrey. *And the wind is offshore too, so it's filling the sails and blowing the ship out to sea. Goodness – it must be going quite fast.*

He paddled on and on, getting quite out of breath. The ship seemed a little nearer now. Yes, it was. He paddled faster. 'Wait, ship, wait! Don't go so fast!'

Now Geoffrey really *was* catching up with the ship. He was almost beside it. Then a wave took it away from him and he paddled furiously, catching it up again. Hurrah – he was up to it! He put down the spade he had been paddling with, and leant over to catch the stern of the ship.

'Got you!' he cried in triumph, and pulled the ship on to the rubber bed. He tied the string round his wrist. 'Now you can't possibly get lost again,' he said. 'I shan't let you!'

He looked round for his spade to paddle back again to shore. It wasn't there! It had gone!

'*Oh!*' wailed Geoffrey. 'The spade's fallen off! I

can't paddle to shore. And the tide's going out, so I'll be taken with it. Oh my goodness, how far off the shore looks now!'

He tried to stand up on the bed and wave for help, but it was too wobbly, and he was afraid of falling overboard. He sat down firmly. 'Well, I'll let you sail again, ship,' he said. 'You can sail behind me – and as I've got your string tied to my wrist, you can't get lost. But it looks as if *I'll* be well and truly lost.'

He sat there on the bobbing rubber bed, feeling scared. The sea looked so very, very big, all round him, heaving up and down all the time. What was going to happen to him? Would he sail on and on for ever? He was hungry already – so goodness knows what he would feel like if he had to spend the night on the water!

Suddenly he heard a throbbing noise. *R-r-r-r-r-r!* *R-r-r-r-r-r!*

Sounds like a motorboat engine! thought Geoffrey,

looking all round. He couldn't see anything at all –
but there was the noise again. *R-r-r-r-r! R-r-r-r-r-r-r!*

He suddenly saw the bow of a rowing boat not far
off. It had an outboard engine, and that was what it
was that was making the noise! Geoffrey yelled and
waved, but the wind blew away his shouts.

'It's seen me! Thank goodness, it's seen me!' said
Geoffrey, as the bow of the boat came nearer, surging
up and down on the waves. Then he heard a shout.

'We're coming! Hang on!'

Geoffrey hung on, his heart beating fast. *What*
a bit of luck that a motorboat should have spotted
him! The boat's outboard engine died a little and
said 'chug-chug-chug' instead of '*r-r-r-r-r-r-r!*'

'Catch, son!' shouted a voice, and Geoffrey saw a
man with a rope in the boat. 'Catch!'

A rope came looping along through the air and
Geoffrey snatched at it. He caught it and held on.

'Tie it round your waist, boy, and then hold tight to
your rubber bed,' shouted the man. 'I'll give you a

tow into shore. You're a little idiot to let yourself float away like this.'

Geoffrey thankfully tied the rope firmly round his waist, still keeping tight hold of the ship's string on his wrist.

'Ready?' yelled the man. 'All set then – hang on!'

And away went the chugging boat, back towards the shore. *R-r-r-r-r-r!* *R-r-r-r-r-r!* And behind it bobbed the rubber bed, with Geoffrey clinging tightly to it – and behind the bed came the old ship!

The beach was crowded with people watching when the boat drew in to shore. Someone there had seen the rubber bed sailing out to sea, and had given the alarm – and out had gone the little motorboat, chugging away to the rescue!

Alan was there too. He was astonished to see the rubber bed, and Geoffrey, and his precious ship sailing furiously behind.

'Your boat is safe!' yelled Geoffrey. 'You needn't worry!'

'I worried about *you*, not my boat,' said Alan. 'What on earth have you been doing, young Geoffrey?'

'Well, don't go for me if I tell you,' said Geoffrey. 'Wait a minute though – I must thank the boatman who rescued me. He was awfully kind.'

What a tale Geoffrey had to tell Alan and the rest! He was surprised when Alan thumped him on the back and said he was a brave kid for going back and getting the rubber bed, and spade, and floating off to find the lovely ship.

'A brave kid – but a bit of an ass too,' said the boatman. 'Don't you lend him that ship of yours again – I might have to go across the Atlantic to rescue him next time!'

'I was jolly scared,' said Geoffrey, 'but you know – it really was quite an adventure!'

Come On, Wags!

Come On, Wags!

'I'M GOING to take Wags for a walk, Mummy!' called Pat. 'I'll be back in good time for tea. Come on, Wags. It's a lovely windy day, just right for a walk!'

Wags ran up, his tail wagging so fast that Pat could hardly see it! 'I never knew a dog with such a waggy tail as you!' he said. 'No wonder we called you Wags. And when you've got your mouth open and your tongue out you look exactly as if you're smiling.'

Wags loved a walk. He didn't mind where he went, so long as he was with Pat. He often wondered why the boy didn't bend down and sniff here and there, to smell all the wonderful smells in the woods, or along the lanes. What a lot Pat was missing!

'You know, Wags, you need a new collar,' said Pat. 'Yours is dreadfully old, and it's really too small for you now. But I simply can't seem to save up enough money to get you a new one. You see, it's always someone's birthday, or else it's Christmas, or else it's holidays by the sea. As soon as I've enough in my moneybox to buy you a collar, I have to spend the money on something else!'

'Wuff, wuff,' said Wags, wagging his tail happily, and smiling up at Pat. What did he care about a new collar? He wasn't a fussy dog at all!

They went through the woods, where all the trees were swaying about in the wind, and came back by the park. Pat stopped at the gates and looked into the park in surprise.

'There must be something on,' he said. 'Look at the crowd of people there, Wags. And there are some tents. Shall we go and see what's happening?'

'Wuff,' answered Wags at once, and scampered into

the park. They soon found out what the show was.

'It's a flower show,' said Pat, 'and a vegetable show too. Well, that's not very interesting to you and me, Wags. But what's in this tent here? I can hear a lot of barking!'

Pat stopped outside the tent and looked at a poster there. 'Dog show!' he said. 'Fancy that! No wonder there's so much barking! Well, I can't put you on show, Wags, old thing – you're just a very, very ordinary dog, even though you are the nicest dog in the world. Come along – we'll go home.'

Wags was disappointed. He would have loved to peep into the dog tent, and say how do you do to the dogs there. He was sure he could hear the bark of Rufus the dog from next door. Perhaps Rufus would win a prize; yes, he was sure to. He was the most beautiful silky spaniel that Wags had ever seen, and very, very haughty towards common little dogs like Wags.

But Pat was already some way away, and Wags

scampered after him. The wind blew his ears back, and ruffled his hairy coat. 'Wuff!' Wags like the wind. It made him feel quite mad, and he leapt about joyfully.

He didn't see a man get up from a nearby seat, holding on to his hat. He rushed right into him, got between the man's legs and bowled him over. Bump! Down the man went, most surprised. He let go of his hat, and the wind pounced down and took it from his head. Whooosh! Away it went, bowling along the path like a live thing, over and over and over!

'Wuff!' Wags gave the man a hurried lick to show he was sorry for knocking him over, and then tore after the hat. Each time he thought he had it, the wind blew a little harder, and Wags simply could not get hold of it.

Away it went, bowling along – down the path, over the grass, across another path and right into the tent where the dog show was being held! And after it went Wags, of course, racing through the tent opening at top speed. The hat came to rest in the middle of the dog ring, and Wags pounced on it joyfully.

He took it into his mouth and then had a look round. Good gracious! What a lot of dogs were in the ring! Big dogs and little ones, fat ones and thin ones, common ones and shining, beautiful ones. Wags sat down in the very middle, the hat still in his mouth. He meant to watch what happened.

Pat appeared in the tent to look for Wags. He was most astonished to see him sitting down right in the middle of the ring, hat in mouth.

'Wags!' he called, but Wags couldn't hear him, there was so much barking.

'Who owns this dog?' shouted a voice. 'Will the owner please come to him?'

Pat stepped into the ring, and went up to Wags. 'Please stay there,' said the man. 'We are about to judge the dogs.'

'But – but my dog isn't . . .' began Pat, and stopped when he saw that nobody was listening to him. 'Here, Wags, we'd better go,' he said. But Wags was not going. This was fun.

Two judges were now going to judge each dog. The dogs were held by their owners, all children. At first Pat couldn't make out how they were being judged – and then he laughed.

'Why, they're judging their tails!' he said. 'Fancy that! Well, I'm afraid you haven't a beautiful tail, Wags, or you might have gone in for such a funny competition!'

But the tails were not being judged for their beauty, or hairiness, or length. They were being judged for their wags! Well, well, well!

'Let me see your dog wag its tail,' said one of the judges to a small girl. She bent down and patted her dog. 'Good dog,' she said, 'good dog!' And, of course, the dog wagged its tail in pleasure. Then the next dog had to wag its tail too, but it was frightened, and put it between its legs! The judges turned to Pat. 'What about your dog?' one said. 'Let us see what kind of wag his tail has.'

Pat stared at the judges in surprise. 'He's got a very waggy tail,' he said, patting Wags. 'Why, we even had to call him Wags! Wags, show what your tail can do! Good dog then, good dog, best dog in the world!'

Wags was so very pleased at being called the best dog in the world in front of so many people that he went nearly mad with delight. He stood there, wagging his tail so fast that it made quite a wind round the judges' legs!

Then he sat down, and thumped his tail on the ground. Thump, thump, THUMP! Thump, thump, THUMP! Everyone began to laugh, because it looked as if Wags was showing off his wagginess in every way he could!

'A very fine wag indeed,' said one of the judges, laughing. 'Wait here, boy. So far your dog has the waggiest tail of all.'

Would you believe it, Wags won the prize! Pat stared in astonishment as the judges came back to Wags and patted him. They handed Pat an envelope.

'Your dog has the most wag in his tail of all the dogs here,' said one. 'He wins the prize. Well done!'

'But – but I didn't really put him in the show,' said Pat. 'It was quite an accident. He didn't . . .'

'Well, accident or not, he's won the prize,' said the judge, laughing. 'Take him away now. We're judging cats next and we want all the dogs well away from here.'

Pat hurried Wags away. At the tent door stood the man whose hat had been blown off. He was looking anxiously around to see if it was anywhere about. Wags had picked it up again and was trotting along with it, looking about for the owner. He dropped it at the man's feet and then rolled over on his back, all four paws in the air.

'That's his way of saying he's sorry he bumped into you and knocked you over, sir,' said Pat, hoping that the man wasn't going to be angry.

'Oh, well, I'll forgive him then,' said the man, brushing the dust from his hat. 'I see he's won a prize. What is he good at, besides knocking people over?'

'He's got the best wag in his tail – better than any other dog's,' said Pat proudly. 'But if he hadn't knocked you over and then run into the tent to get your hat back, he'd never have been in the show at all.'

'Well, I'm glad I've been of some use to you,' said the man, putting on his hat. 'Congratulations, dog, on being such a fine tail-wagger!'

Pat went off with Wags. He stopped under a tree to open the envelope. Good gracious! There were four half crowns there! They had felt rather like four *pennies* to him when he had held them in the envelope.

'Wags! Your tail has won you ten shillings,' he said. 'Enough to buy you a new collar – and to get Mother and you and me some ice cream for tea. Come on – we'll go and spend it!'

So away they went, Wags bounding along and

wagging his tail faster than ever. What an afternoon!
He was sorry Pat hadn't a tail to wag too!

The Bubble
Airships

The Bubble Airships

ONCE UPON a time, when Jack took his bubble blower and bowl of soapy water into the garden, he had a strange adventure. He sat down by the old oak tree, mixed up his water and began to blow big rainbow bubbles.

The adventure began when one of the bubbles floated upwards and disappeared inside the big hole in the middle of the old oak tree. Jack watched it go there – and no sooner had he seen it pop inside the tree than he heard a great many excited little voices coming from the tree itself!

The little boy listened in astonishment. Who could

be inside the tree? He climbed up and peeped inside – but it was too dark to see anything, and as soon as the little folk inside heard him climbing up, they kept quite quiet. Not a word could he hear!

This is a funny thing, thought Jack in excitement. *I must get my torch and light up the hollow in the tree – then I may see something lovely!*

He ran to get his torch. He climbed up the tree once more and shone his torch into the hole – and there, at the very bottom of the old tree, deep down inside the hollow trunk, Jack saw a crowd of tiny, frightened pixies, all looking up at him with pale, scared faces!

The little boy stared in amazement. He had never in his life seen a pixie before – and here were about twenty, all squeezed up together!

'What are you doing inside this tree?' he asked. 'Do you live here?'

The pixies chattered together in high, twittering voices. 'Shall we tell him, shall we tell him?' they cried.

Then one of the pixies looked up at Jack and said, 'Little boy, you have a kind face. We will tell you why we are here. The green goblins caught us yesterday and cut off our wings. They wanted us to tell them all the magic spells we knew, and because we wouldn't they shut us up in this hollow tree.'

'But why can't you get out?' asked Jack.

'Well, our wings are gone,' said the pixie sorrowfully, 'so we can't fly – and the tree is much too difficult to climb inside – so here we are, prisoners, and the goblins will come again tonight to try to make us tell them what we know.'

'I'm sorry about your wings,' said Jack. 'Won't you ever be able to fly again?'

'Oh yes,' said another pixie. 'They will grow again – but not for four weeks.'

'What were you so excited about just now?' asked Jack. 'I was blowing bubbles when I suddenly heard you chattering away in here, and that's what made me come and look.'

'Well, one of your bubbles suddenly blew down into the tree,' said a pixie. 'And it gave us such a surprise. We grabbed at it – but it broke and made us all wet!'

'I wish I could get you out,' said Jack. 'But I can't possibly reach down to you – the tree is so big, and you are right at the bottom.'

'No, I'm afraid we shall have to stay locked up here,' said the pixies sadly.

But suddenly one of the pixies gave a shout and cried, 'I know! Could the little boy blow some bubbles down into the tree for us? Because if he could, we might make some buckets of grass and fix them to the bubbles – get into the baskets and float off!'

'Good idea!' shouted everyone. 'Little boy, will you do it?'

'Yes, rather!' cried Jack. 'I'll go and pick you some grass first. Then you can be weaving little baskets of it while I fetch my soapy water and my bubble blower. I shall have to be careful not to spill the water when I climb up the tree!'

In a short while Jack had picked some grass and dropped it down to the pixies. They at once began to weave strong little baskets with their tiny fingers – baskets quite big and strong enough to carry them away! Jack climbed down again and picked up his water and bubble blower. Very carefully he climbed up the tree once more, holding his bowl of water in one hand, and pulling himself up the tree with the other.

He carried his bubble blower in his mouth, so that was quite safe. He switched on his torch and looked down into the tree again. The pixies had made some beautiful baskets, with long blades of grass sticking up from them for ropes.

'You will be able to make lovely airships with those baskets hung beneath my bubbles,' cried the little boy. He blew a big blue and green bubble and puffed it into the tree. A small pixie held up his green basket to it as it floated down. The grass caught on to the soapy bubble and the basket swung there, just like the underneath of an airship! The pixie climbed into it, and the others gave him a gentle push. Off he floated up the tree, and as soon as he came out into the sunshine, Jack blew the bubble away from the leaves and branches so that it would not burst. It floated gently to the ground and burst there with a little pop!

The pixie tumbled out of the basket on to the ground, laughing in delight to think he had escaped from the tree.

Jack blew some more big bubbles, and they floated down the hole in the tree. Some of them burst before they reached the pixies, for they bumped against the sides of the tree, but those that reached the bottom had the grass buckets fixed to them in a trice – and then up came the pixies, each in their own little bubble airship!

Jack laughed to see them. They really did look funny, floating along in their tiny airships. The last pixie of all had no one to push him out of the hollow tree and he broke two or three bubbles trying to push himself off; but at last he managed to float upwards too, and soon he was on the grass with the others, laughing and talking in excitement.

'We shall run away to a rabbit hole we know and hide there till our wings have grown,' said a pixie to Jack. 'It's so kind of you to have helped us. Goodbye! We may see you again some day! Won't those goblins be angry tonight when they find we have gone!'

They all ran off and left Jack alone with his bubble blower. How excited he was to think of his strange adventure with it! Who would have thought that he could blow bubble airships?

The pixies rewarded Jack for his kindness. They found out where his little garden was, and they kept it well weeded and well watered for him, and made his flowers the biggest and loveliest in the garden. I know, because I have seen them!

Acknowledgements

All efforts have been made to seek necessary permissions. The stories in this publication first appeared in the following publications:

'The Silver Merman' first appeared in *Sunny Stories for Little Folks*, No. 67, 1929.

'In the Heart of the Wood' first appeared in *The Enid Blyton Holiday Book*, 1946. Syndicated story.

'A Cat in Fairyland' first appeared in *Sunny Stories for Little Folks*, No. 124, 1931.

'Mr Pippin's Lemonade' first appeared in *Let's Read*, 1933.

'The Jackdaw Afternoon' first appeared in *Enid Blyton's Magazine*, No. 9, Vol. 2, 1954.

'A Real Fairy Fair' first appeared in *The Teachers World*, No. 902, 1922.

'The Very Brave Puppy' first appeared in *Sunny Stories for Little Folks*, No. 128, 1931.

'The Little Domino House' first appeared in *Sunny Stories for Little Folks*, No. 130, 1931.

'Sailor Jim's Telescope' first appeared in *Enid Blyton's Sunny Stories*, No. 498, 1951.

'Jinky the Jumping Frog' first appeared in *Sunny Stories for Little Folks*, No. 162, 1933.

'The Three Chocolate Bears' first appeared in *Sunny Stories for Little Folks*, No. 145, 1932.

'Mary Brown and Mary Contrary' first appeared in *Sunny Stories for Little Folks*, No. 161, 1933.

'Adventure in the Afternoon' first appeared in *Enid Blyton's Sunny Stories*, No. 437, 1948.

'Tommy's White Duck' first appeared in *Enid Blyton's Sunny Stories*, No. 107, 1939.

'The Girl Who Was Left Behind' first appeared in *Enid Blyton's Sunny Stories*, No. 358, 1945.

ACKNOWLEDGEMENTS

'Adventure for Two' first appeared in *Enid Blyton's Sunny Stories*, No. 466, 1949.

'The Land of Nowhere' first appeared in *Sunny Stories for Little Folks*, No. 175, 1933.

'The Train that Broke in Half' first appeared in *Enid Blyton's Sunny Stories*, No. 220, 1941.

'Belinda All Alone' first appeared in *Sunny Stories for Little Folks*, No. 144, 1932.

'Granny's Lovely Necklace' first appeared in *Enid Blyton's Sunny Stories*, No. 28, 1937.

'Cowardy Custard' first appeared in *Sunny Stories for Little Folks*, No. 197, 1934.

'Good Gracious Me!' first appeared in *Enid Blyton's Sunny Stories*, No. 354, 1945.

'Quite an Adventure' first appeared in *Enid Blyton's Magazine*, No. 15, Vol. 6, 1958.

'Come On, Wags!' first appeared in *Enid Blyton's Magazine*, No. 26, Vol. 5, 1957.

'The Bubble Airships' first appeared in *Enid Blyton's Sunny Stories*, No. 42, 1937.

Enid Blyton

is one of the most popular children's authors of all time. Her books have sold over 500 million copies and have been translated into other languages more often than any other children's author.

Enid Blyton adored writing for children. She wrote over 600 books and hundreds of short stories. *The Famous Five* books, now 75 years old, are her most popular. She is also the author of other favourites including *The Secret Seven*, *The Magic Faraway Tree*, *Malory Towers* and *Noddy*.

Born in London in 1897, Enid lived much of her life in Buckinghamshire and adored dogs, gardening and the countryside. She was very knowledgeable about trees, flowers, birds and animals. Dorset – where some of the Famous Five's adventures are set – was a favourite place of hers too.

Enid Blyton's stories are read and loved by millions of children (and grown-ups) all over the world. Visit enidblyton.co.uk to discover more.